The Disappearance of
Rory Brophy

The Disappearance of Rory Brophy

CARL LOMBARD

Carl Lombard

FOURTH ESTATE · *London*

First published in Great Britain in 1992 by
Fourth Estate Limited
289 Westbourne Grove
London W11 2QA

A catalogue record for this book is available from the
British Library

ISBN 1-85702-036-7

Typeset by York House Typographic Ltd, London W7.
Printed in Great Britain by Biddles Ltd., Guildford and
King's Lynn

For Robbie

Contents

1   *The Flyover*

On a Thursday afternoon, poor Rory Brophy walked up the road until he was standing in the middle of the flyover looking down at the trucks whizzing beneath him. Whenever one went by, the wind almost knocked him over and it made him dizzy to look at them coming down at sixty or seventy miles an hour and then disappearing underneath him. He watched one emerge on the crest of the hill ahead and followed its course as it approached.

As he did so, he climbed over the railings and stood on the very edge of the concrete until only his heels supported him. When he guessed that the truck was twenty yards away – a figure which he had deduced to be significant by a crazy algorithm – he closed his eyes, leaned forward and let gravity take its course. In his right hand he held a piece of paper which read 'I've had enough, I'm going'. Indeed he had had enough and he was going, but not where he thought, for the flaw in the algorithm revealed itself and instead of falling beneath the truck, he landed in the back of it on top of a mound of satsumas. He was on his way to the port at Sion, and from there to Sweden. In his later life he would thank God for satsumas and I will tell you about that. But first there is the question of the sun, the wind, the light, the noise, the concrete, and all of these as they affected Cavendish Road.

I begin, sitting in the front garden of my grandfather's house. It was summertime, old summertime, when the weather was always good and warm. It was also midday. I know this because my mother always took me there at midday when she brought the old man his dinner because she was such a good cook and he was such a terrible one. Before we had left home, I had eaten my own dinner despite her advice that I should wait and eat with grandfather, advice which I had rejected because I could never put off the task of eating her food. This day that I am speaking about, I had been playing 'wheelbarrows' in the back garden with Eglund Bowe. Eglund Bowe perpetually suffered from head colds, so whenever we played this game his nose discharged a clear fluid which quickly solidified in trails on the grass as if left by some giant snail with a belly full of poison. Whenever his mother came to see if he had been with me, my own mother would only have to go into the garden and examine the grass for the silvery trails. This particular day we were not alone in the garden – Rory Brophy was there as well. When my mother came out to call me for my dinner, Rory drooped his shoulders as he always did at such times, and left for home and his mother's chronic rabbit-stew. After I had eaten, we set off to bring grandfather his meal. I held it in my hands wrapped in a dishcloth, and despite having just finished my own meal, I was hungry again by the time I had to hand it over to him.

My grandfather's house was the last one at the end

of the street. The houses were quite old, maybe eighty years or so. My mother had been born in the box-room at the front. It was the smaller of the two bedrooms, and I remember her bringing me into it one day and telling me that it was where she had been born. She said that it was very important to her that she knew exactly, and I mean to the nearest square yard, the spot where she had first arrived. Whenever there was trouble she would go to the box-room and sit for some time on one of the chairs that were stored up there. It was not because she wanted to be alone and the room was the only place on the street where it was possible. In fact the opposite was the case. She went there to be with someone – her own mother, who had died a long time ago and was buried in the cemetery at Crevit. My mother rarely went to the grave except on anniversaries and at Christmas. I don't think she derived any solace from it. Not nearly as much as she did from going to the box-room and sitting in the yardage of her birth, right at the spot where it had happened. She pitied people born in hospitals who could never get that thrill of returning again and again to where their lives had started.

When the houses were built, my grandfather's was the last one. Beyond it there was a field where cattle grazed, and beyond that again, Dempsey Road and its smelly tyre factory. Ten years before however, the field disappeared and was replaced by a main road which ran at right angles to ours. We all got used to the noise of the traffic as we had to. The protests which followed the announcement that the huge road was to be built all came to nothing, and the residents committee, set up to organise our anger, melted away in the honoured fashion that planners have always understood. Now you could wander a few feet from the spot where my mother was born and be standing in the middle of the busiest road you could care to imagine. The road had been built and there was nothing we could do about it. We had acclimatised, we had evolved, we had changed the colour of our skin as camouflage. Our ears had grown accustomed to the noise. We had convinced ourselves that there was life after progress, and reassured ourselves that we could still go to my grandfather's garden in the summer and relax in the sumptuous heat.

He ate his bacon and egg pie and I sat and envied him. He talked to my mother and when they were finished he turned his attention to me and began the ancient story of Troy. As the men descended to the ground by rope, their progress was unexpectedly halted. Missus Brophy was shouting something. We all looked down the road and there she was. Running up towards us waving a sheet of paper in her hand looking like Neville Chamberlain. Not in looks, mind you, although she did have a modicum of hair on her lip, but in the way that he had once drawn everyone's attention to a slip of paper in his hand as if it held the future of all that was known. 'Have you seen it?' she was shouting. She was a huge woman. How she could have conceived a shrimp like Rory was a mystery of genetics. Her massive breasts waved from right to left way out in front of her. 'Did you see this?' she said again as she came into the garden. My mother took the piece of paper and read it. It had the letterhead of the City Council on it and began with the words 'Dear Resident'.

The letter told us that the Council was to debate building a flyover diagonally across the main road to link the airport with the city centre. It would come from the left-hand side of Dempsey Road as we looked across at it, and run along the back of my grandfather's house. When he read the letter, the old man looked up at the sky where the proposed construction would go. He panned his head as he followed its course until it disappeared behind the house. He could find few words to speak. He started a few sentences, but was unable to finish them. He pointed at the letter and up to the sky and back down to the letter again. By now more angry people had arrived and huddled sessions had begun, so I slipped away to see Rory.

They tell me that what happened was almost the same as had taken place ten years before when the first 'Dear Resident' letters arrived with the good news about the main road. As happened then, it was Missus Brophy who took it upon herself to mobilise people. She called a meeting in her house and so many people turned up that most of them had to stand in the garden and listen in through the opened window. As is so often the case at such gatherings, there was an immediate call to set up a committee. Nominations were sought and Missus Brophy's name was put forward to loud applause. After the mandatory expressions of self-doubt as to her qualifications to be the Secretary of the Committee, she happily accepted. The resounding applause for her acceptance speech had barely died when a man stepped forward from the crowd and asked leave to introduce himself. He was young, perhaps in his early thirties, and very handsome. He wore a dapper grey suit and a green tie which offset his magnificent tan (it was the old summers). His hair was jet-black and sleaked back with gel, and his presence immediately attracted

5

attention because no one of such excellent appearance had ever lived near us. The crowd fell silent in wonder at who he was. 'I am Cathal Callaghan,' he said without any signs of doubt, 'and I am a Democratic Justice Party City Councillor.' At that moment, Missus Brophy's lifetime collection of foreign dolls and cut-glass almost came to an end. For the Democratic Justice Party was the party of government; and, more relevant to this story, it was the largest party on the City Council. There was uproar. A number of people moved forward in a menacing fashion, but the speaker quietened the noise and stopped all move-ment by raising the palms of his hands which were brilliant white in comparison with the rest of his visible skin. He shook his head from side to side and cried, 'Wait a minute, wait a minute.' There was silence again. 'I'm with you, I'm with you,' he contin-ued. 'I disagree with this plan. I come from an area just like this and I know that this flyover will destroy the place, that's why I'm going to vote against it and that means there will be stalemate.' There was silence and then there was uproar. This time it was happy uproar. The dolls and cut-glass were replaced on the shelves, and Mister Callaghan received multitudinous slaps on the back which made his face go a worrying shade of red.

This was a famous case. The Democratic Justice Party had always been the party of loyalty and ranks were never broken. What the party decided was that no one, least of all a mere councillor, should ever go against the hegemony. That was why this was so sensational. The national press were as astounded as everyone else with Mister Callaghan. They descended on the street, which became the centre of the nation's attention. My grandfather's house was on television and in the newspapers. My mother marvelled that the window of the room where she had been born was being seen by the whole country. On the evening news they showed our street. When they came to film we all jostled to get our faces in front of the lens. I believe I saw myself in the top right-hand corner of the screen just for a fleeting moment as the camera panned the street. It was not possible to say conclusively that it was me for I was unable to find anyone who could support the sighting, which happened as the reporter was saying that this case would make history. I jumped out of my chair and shouted, 'There, there, that was me!' But when I sought witnesses the next day I found none – no one had seen it. But I truly believe it was me. I appeared during the 'his' of 'history', and it has remained one of my favourite words ever since.

There were many predictions that Cathal Callaghan would not go ahead with his threat to defy the party. Reporters and politicians said he wouldn't, while everyone on our street prayed he would. The Council met on a wet Wednesday night in October. We were all there outside the building with placards telling them to save our community. We hissed at them as they went in. Only Cathal Callaghan received a tumultuous welcome. He was shielded from the rain in case his suit got wet. He had his back slapped again and again. He even gave us a speech outside the building, and when he went inside he proved a man of his word when he voted down the Justice Party. The flyover would not go ahead. We all went home with the air in the city carrying a heavy scent of the Prime Minister's rage, but that did not concern us.

In Missus Brophy's front room, where the campaign had begun, the adults drank alcohol and the rest of us had tea. Many toasts were made. In particular we toasted our hero, Cathal Callaghan. We toasted his nice suits and his jet-black hair. His tanned skin and his superb command of our language. We toasted defectors of all shades because they made life interesting. 'He's a one hundred per cent hunk,' said a woman. 'He's more than that, he's a hundred and ten per cent hunk,' said another. 'He's more again,' said someone else, 'he's a hunk and a half.' 'He's gorgeous.' 'He's not only gorgeous, he's great as well. He's great and gorgeous.' If this was the lot of the defector, then I wanted to be one immediately. With such adulation to look forward to, I wondered why it had taken so long for someone to break ranks with the party. What I was not to know at that time, what we were all oblivious to as we sang and made toasts in Missus Brophy's front room that night, was that we had not heard the last of the matter. As I sat and pondered the glorious existence of the defector, and as the women praised his beauty, knives were being drawn from their sheaths down at the Justice Party's headquarters. The Chairman and the Prime Minister spent much of the night on the phone to each other. The Party Secretary later wrote in his boring memoirs that that night saw the beginning of the horrendous duodenal ulcer which brought about such a late end to an awful career. The Chief Press Secretary scribbled an illegible resignation note which he only handed to the Chairman after several unsuccessful attempts to slip it into his pocket without being noticed. When he looked at it, the Chairman had to refer it back to the author because he couldn't read it, and when the

Press Secretary explained that he couldn't face the media the following morning, the Chairman accepted the message and then broke his subordinate's nose with a dictionary.

What fall-out there was. The cameras came back to Cavendish Road and Cathal Callaghan told people of what he believed would be the personal consequences of his actions. His chances of ever leading the party had not only gone, but there was every probability that he would be thrown out. 'He can't have his cake and eat it,' said one party official. This was the first time I had heard this phrase and, although I didn't understand it, it sounded excellent to me – which was just as well because it became the phrase of the controversy. Cathal Callaghan fought his corner like the man we knew him to be, refusing to accept that he had done anything wrong. 'There are times when loyalty must take second place,' he said, and we on Cavendish Road were fortunate that ours was such an occasion.

But the Prime Minister was furious with the gorgeous upstart. He didn't show it in public, but he was not prepared to be beaten by a freshman who was still searching for his mother's nipple when he, the Prime Minister, was killing colonialist troops and living as a fugitive in the days before independence. Cathal Callaghan would not get off so lightly as simply to be thrown out of the party and enter the history books as the man who defied the father of the nation. There would be no such retrospective for the tanned man with the gay suits. 'There is no such creature as a Justice Party defector,' the Prime Minister later wrote, 'there are simply those who prefer the chicane to the straight road.' The Prime Minister's greatest wish in the wake of the Council vote was to see the rebel return to the fold . . . Then he would throw him out.

Cavendish Road was indeed a place of mixed fortunes where to some were given all the good times, to others all the bad, and to others again a combination of both. In this third category there was Julie Davitt, who was in her teens and still on the attractive side of beautiful when the rest of us were consumed with the question of the flyover. She liked to read love-stories because they reminded her of the most precious thing she had. This was both invisible and untouchable. Even she had never seen it. She did not know what it smelt like nor had she any concept of its shape or its size, and yet she took it with her wherever she went. It was as much a part of her as her arms. This thing was her image of Manfred Talbot which she nourished with her attention. It was an image, mind you, not a memory. It had to be an image for there had never been such a person as Manfred Talbot. He was, as they say, a figment of her imagination which never pro- gressed to the level of mental picture and certainly not to the shimmering glimpse of a midnight apparition. She had no idea of what he looked like or how tall he was. There was only one thing of which she was sure and that was that his skin was white. As you have probably guessed, Julie Davitt was an inveterate dreamer. She lived in a world of her own, immune to what went on around her. She only made contact with the rest of us for mundane things like eating. It was an experience to try to talk to her. She would be pleasant for a while as you asked if she wanted to go and catch wasps. She would begin to answer that that would be a good . . . And then you would get the distinct feeling that she was no longer aware of your presence. Her head would tilt to one side and a slight smile would come to her face. You would know that he was behind you, invisible to everyone else and formless even to her, and so you would forget about the wasps and leave the two of them to it.

When her father was in a good mood he called her 'Head-in-the-Clouds', when he wasn't he called her 'Stupid'. He chastised her for her day-dreaming. 'Grow up girl,' he would say, 'this day-dreaming won't get you anywhere. The day is long gone when a woman could afford not to worry about getting a good job. A man expects his woman to be able to contribute financially to the house now. How will you be able to do that if you don't get a good job? Do you want to end up wiping the canteen tables in the tyre factory or cleaning the floors in the Brilliant Bakery, with every son-of-a-bitch security man slapping your backside and whistling after you to go to bed with him? Is that what you want? So go and get yourself a good education. Remember, education is power. Men don't slap the backsides of women with university degrees.'

On an evening when Cavendish Road was still very newsworthy, Julie wandered into the living room where her mother and father were watching the television news. The girl sat at the table by the door. She could just about remember that Cavendish Road was where she lived, but the whole flyover episode had gone over her head (forgive the pun). This was all news to her. She was momentarily back in the land of the living. She listened as the newscaster spoke of the continuing trouble over the vote. His comments were followed by an item which began with a reporter standing outside the house of Cathal Callaghan. Out came the defector and he stopped to speak to the newsman. 'What will you do if they try to expel you from the party?' he was asked. He had no time to answer before Julie jumped from her chair and started shouting at the television. 'Manfred, Manfred, it's you, you're here.' At first her father told her to shut up. Then he realised something peculiar was happening. His daughter was yelling some wild name at a man on the television. 'What are you on about?' he shouted at her. 'Who the hell is Manfred?' Julie Davitt did not answer. Realising that in a fleeting moment she had given away her secret, she ran from the room and the house and down the road, leaving her father standing in complete amazement in his living room. Her mother looked at him and he back at her and they were both thinking, Head-in-the-Clouds has really flipped it this time.

A narrow lane ran off Cleavor Street along the backs of gardens. Few people ever went down it. It smelt of wet cats and there was a lot of rubbish in it: bins and boxes and always a pile of cardboard containers with the Sunburst Oranges label on them. It was behind these that Julie Davitt crouched. Well down so no one could see her, she thought about her predicament. Although she had never seen the face of Manfred Talbot she had always known that some day she would. She knew that when the time came he would make himself known to her. Both of their movements were controlled by destiny, which would not allow their paths to cross until the time was right. And now the time had come – sooner than expected, which was why she had been so surprised, but it was him. He had been revealed to her.

The phone rang at the headquarters of the Justice Party and Annabella Fogarty answered it. She tried to disguise the bad case of Chinese flu she had contracted in France. Being careful not to sniffle down the line, she asked the caller if she could be of assistance.

Annabella Fogarty was part of the Prime Minister's recent drive to improve the party's wretched public relations. After stepping out of the wrong side of bed one morning, he arrived at headquarters and immediately demanded that the porter be brought to his office. The old man, who had been in his job for twenty years (though he'd never once voted for his employers), had never had an experience like it. The Chief was furious with him and demanded to know why there were no flags flying over the building. 'There should be two flags up there,' he roared at the porter, 'the national flag and the party flag. All I see are naked poles. Now get me the flags here at once.' Within a few minutes the fearful porter had returned with two filthy, creased rags in his arms. He couldn't even look at the Chief, and he grimaced as he waited for his reaction to the state of the material. He was ordered to lay them on the floor, one on top of the other, and asked if he would sleep between sheets that were so dirty. He could only answer 'No, sir.' (The truth was he never used sheets anyway.) He was instructed to have the flags washed and ironed, and warned that if the Chief ever entered the building again without them flapping in the breeze above his head, he would be sacked.

Then there was the condition of the building itself. The facade was dishevelled and badly needed new paint. The Chief ordered a letter to be sent to the ten newest party recruits inviting them to come and meet him personally. Within days this special audience was held. The Chief took them into his office, where he personally poured them tea and offered some of his favourite biscuits. While they drank, they chatted about their ambitions in politics and their loyalty to the party. They were congratulated by the Chief for their youthful energy and vision. 'Thank God for youth,' he said, and then broke the news that they could show no greater loyalty than to volunteer to paint the front of the building with materials they could pick up from the porter's office on the way out.

Next there was the telephonist. That she was a problem was brought to the Chief's attention on an occasion when he rang the Press Secretary from his Prime Ministerial office. It was hard to believe, but this was the first time he had ever personally called the headquarters. What greeted him on the other end of the line shocked him to his socks: a voice that sounded like a fork against the bottom of a saucepan. He had to hold the receiver away from his ear . . . this woman had to go. Auditions were held and a shortlist of five was selected. Each was seated in turn at the reception desk in the foyer of the party headquarters. The Prime Minister made five consecutive phone calls and decided that the fourth was the voice they needed. That was Annabella Fogarty, who now asked the caller if she could be of assistance.

On the other end of the line was the timid voice of a young woman who asked if she might have the address of Cathal Callaghan so that she could write to him to express her disapproval of his disloyalty. The very mention of his name was a shock to the building.

At that moment everyone inside felt a shiver run through their bones. They braced themselves and turned up the heating. Unaware of the real cause, they went pale and briskly shook their heads to create some friction. Annabella Fogarty asked the caller to wait a moment. She returned with the information and gladly gave it – any enemy of Cathal Callaghan was a friend of the party.

Head-in-the-Clouds scribbled the address on the top of the fifth page of the *Daily Sentinel*, just above the headline 'MAN KILLS WIFE WITH BLOW FROM BAG OF FLOUR'. In the centre of the city there was a place where religious preachers gathered to ask people to repent and be saved. The penniless students from the Municipal College of Artistic Endeavour also went there to draw the faces of Botticelli and Titian on the pavement. A statue of the Second Count of Panap had once stood nearby, but had been pulled down on the night of The Revolution of the New Day (also known as The Great Awakening). In its place was erected a street map for the assistance of tourists. Head-in-the-Clouds stood in front of the map looking for the street which contained the house of the beautiful dissident, whom we must temporarily call Manfred Talbot. She found it in reference square E4, a place by the name of Carmichael Square.

Two hundred years ago, cattle roamed where Carmichael Square now stood. It then became the site for a fancy new square for the colonialists. Fine houses were built around it and, in the middle, a grand garden was laid out. Nature was shaped and moulded by men who didn't like the way it looked. The houses were fine indeed and lived in by professionals. That was up until the night of The Great Awakening, when

15

all those who lived there were ordered to hand the property over to the state or have it confiscated by large men. It set legal history by becoming a jurisdiction of its own. Laws were passed which applied only to the square. It became an example to all that the revolution had taken place and that things would never be the same again.

No one was allowed to live there any more. Those few colonialists who refused to relinquish their property voluntarily were hauled out and resettled on the newly named Avenue of the Vanquished and the ancient square returned to nature. The facades of the buildings were battered by the wind and rain and there was no one to refurbish them. The gardens ran wild and vermin took over the houses, which became more unmagnificent with every day that passed.

In one of the rooms where the colonial judges had once spent their evenings discussing jurisprudence in the age of rebellion there did now, however, live the brothers Cussons. They had left normal society on the day that Big Steph, a practitioner of dubious medicine in the slums of Preece, told them that identical twins were proof of the presence of evil in the world. An identical twin was only half a person with half a soul, which had been tampered with in the womb and divided like a worm so both ends grew. Thereafter rejected by their mother, who was a devotee of Big Steph, they survived by sifting through the bins of the hotels on the streets around Saint John Bosco and along the seafront at Yivon.

They never found out if Big Steph's diagnosis had any truth in it. Instead they protected themselves by never being seen in public together. Their minds succumbed to the stories they had been told by the

huge woman of Preece about the tradition of inciner-
ating identicals at the stake in the wake of the death of
a child, so they lived at alternate times of the day – one
venturing out at sunrise, the other at sunset, but never
both at the same time.

It was during a daytime excursion, some years after
the revolution, that Ignatius Cussons came across the
'No Entry' sign at Carmichael Square and, in the best
traditions of illiteracy, entered. He found himself
alone in the square. Like a body on arrival in Heaven
he stood with his eyes and his mouth wide open. He
walked up the ten steps to the door of number 79 and
pushed against the wooden structure, which opened
in front of him. The house was completely empty –
even the carved end of the banisters had been sawn
off. But Ignatius Cussons saw only one thing. Like a
young man experiencing love at first sight, he almost
cried out with joy. Looking straight up above he saw
what he had dreamed of – a roof without holes in it.
His discovery was given an approving second opinion
by Justin Cussons during his night outing, and within
twenty-four hours they had moved into their new
home.

In the lanes of Fontaineau where the tramps slept
every night, the absence of the Cussons brothers was
not given much attention at first. People often disappeared for days and nothing was thought of it. There
was a rule of thumb to the effect that if someone went
missing for two weeks, nothing would be said or
done. They could have been in a minor accident or
picked up by one of the religious orders. If they were
missing for more than two weeks, they were presumed to have found somewhere else to live, or
to have died. Four weeks passed without anyone

seeing the Cussons brothers. On the third Tuesday in November, Ignatius Cussons was picking through the bins in Yivon. This was one of the best days of the year for it. It was the day after Union Day, when the nation celebrated the unification of the forces of the north and south in the great fight against the colonialists. It was always celebrated on the third Monday in November and the entire preceding weekend was a holiday. It became very fashionable to spend the weekend in one of the big hotels along the beach at Yivon and attend the barbecues. On the morning after, when all of the sore heads had gone back to work, the tramps came out. Ignatius Cussons was filling a plastic bag with three bread rolls which had been untouched by human teeth when he was seen by a fellow tramp from his old home in Fontaineau. Ignatius was unaware that he had been seen and, when he had gathered as much as he could carry, he returned to Carmichael Square and led his follower to it. Within a day, the tramps of Fontaineau had become the tramps of Carmichael Square, where they spent their nights singing and drinking. It was during one of these nights that a fire got out of control when a bottle of kerosene was broken during a fight. Half of the square went up in flames. No one ever knew who or how many died in it, but the inferno was another turning-point in the history of the place.

The fire occurred at a time of heated debate (unforgivable pun) amongst the architectural fraternity over the merits of classicism, modernism and post-modernism, and Carmichael Square was the fulcrum for the debate. At the Institute of Accountable Architects, the young souls of post-modernism were in the ascendancy. The President of the Institute was also the brother-in-law of the Chief Secretary of the Department of the Administration, whose brief included buildings. In the offices of the Department, the Minister was persuaded by his faithful Secretary that the laws on Carmichael Square were childish and out of date. The Minister agreed and repealed them. Tenders were invited for the job of creating a new square. The decision was taken by the civil servants in the Department that the best design was that of the architects Mansell and Gogarty. They were disciples of post-modernism. By coincidence, Mister Gogarty owned a yacht often frequented by the Minister's brother, but I mention this in passing and make no allegation that anything about this episode smelt in the least of dead fish. William Travis Casper put up the money for the development and Carmichael Square returned to being one of the most fashionable areas of the city.

Mister Casper was a man who believed in a quick return on his investments. The rents in Carmichael Square were high and only those holding well-paid jobs could even consider taking a house there. It was a triumph of the new architectural school. The new houses were magnificent and the garden in the centre of the square was replaced by a plaza with wooden benches and small pots of flowers. In the warm evenings it was a lovely place to sit and read. The rest of the city could not be seen from it. In number 79, where the Cussons brothers had first arrived and set in motion the events which led to their probable cremation, now lived none other than Cathal Callaghan, or Manfred Talbot.

There were no buses that passed via Carmichael Square as the residents would have considered it an insult. The nearest stop was a few hundred yards away and it was from here that Head-in-the-Clouds began the last leg of her journey to the home of Manfred Talbot. When she arrived at the door of number 79, she rang the bell and waited, but no one came to answer. She found the door at the rear was locked as well, so she broke the glass with a rock and let herself in. The house was beautiful inside. The living room was L-shaped and had two levels. A spiral staircase in the centre of the room led upstairs. Head-in-the-Clouds took the stairs and walked about in the largest bedroom, which had all the signs of being used by Manfred Talbot.

At thirteen minutes to twelve, he arrived home. He was tired, but when he turned on the light in his bedroom he immediately noticed the bulge beneath the blankets on his bed. Thinking that it could only be Maria Osterban, the waitress from the Paragon of Virtue night-club, he turned off the light, undressed and got into bed. He was of the opinion that no woman could have greater pleasure than being woken in the night by the groping hands of a handsome dissident squeezing her breasts. He searched for the organs of his bed-friend and when he found them he was certain that this was not Maria Osterban – she was much bigger than this. He jumped from his bed as he wasn't sure if the person sharing it were male or female. It could have been the drummer with the homosexual band The Freelance Faggots – which played every Tuesday and Thursday at the Paragon of Virtue – who had expressed an interest in sleeping with the tanned crusader on many occasions. Manfred Talbot raced across the bedroom searching for his trousers and the light switch (in that order). When both were on he yelled at the slumbering hill to reveal itself.

Head-in-the-Clouds woke up and rubbed her eyes. She was momentarily confused, but the sight of her most precious possession brought her back to her senses (I use the phrase cautiously). She stood up and held out her arms to him. She was completely naked. The dissident thought he was dreaming as she kept calling him Manfred. Terrified at the tender age of the girl before him, he ran down the stairs – followed closely by the girl, who was still calling him by this strange name. She wanted to know what was wrong with him and why he would not come to bed. Head-in-the-Clouds cornered him in the kitchen and put her arms around his waist to hug him. He was petrified and could hardly breathe with disbelief. Eventually he broke free and walked to the far end of the room running his hand through his jet-black hair. 'Who . . . Who are you? And what are you doing here?' he said to her. 'Manfred, it's me,' she said moving closer to him. Her voice held a worried note and she was half crying at his rejection of her. 'It's me, Manfred. Please come to bed.' By this time he had had enough. 'You're nuts, you are, you are crazy. You ought to get your chimney cleaned out. You're getting out of here.' He raced upstairs to get her clothes and threw them to her before going into the living room and closing the door behind him. When she was dressed, she went to join him. He sat with his back to her. ' How did you get in here?' he said. 'I broke in,' was the reply. 'Great, so I've been burgled as well. You'd better leave the way you came. Now go on, get out of here.' Knowing she had been rejected but not understanding why, Head-in-the-Clouds left by the back door and wandered the streets, her stomach physically hurting with loneliness.

Cathal Callaghan went to bed shaking his head in disbelief at what had happened. All of the lights were out at number 79, but not so across the square at 112. It was the former residence of Jason Chilcott (the Melon Mogul) who used to come to town in the old days and spend parts of his evenings sitting in his bedroom buggering a wine-coloured bowling ball. In the room where sport and sex had been so unusually inter-twined, there was a man with a grin packing things into a case. The man was Lawrence Gross, and what he was packing was photographic equipment, includ-ing a lens the length of a drainpipe. 'So powerful it could spot a man going bald five years before it started to happen,' he would say. These were lucrative times for Lawrence Gross. He no longer worked for the easy-credit companies who employed him as a debt collector on five per cent of whatever he recovered. Now he was under the patronage of the Chief. First, he had worked as a party thug who would stuff burning paper into hostile ballot boxes; now, though, he had moved on to more subtle endeavours.

The Chief had recognised in Lawrence Gross a quality which he knew to be essential for an under-cover surveillance man. That quality was patience, and Lawrence Gross had it in abundance. It was not that he recognised it as a virtue in itself, but simply that he was afraid to return to his mentor and report a failure. This time he had struck gold. He had the pictorial koh-i-noor on a spool of film. He had photo-graphed a nubile young girl entering the house of the dissident, undressing in the bedroom and getting into bed; also, the arrival of the dissident, his joining her in the bedroom, his sharing the same bed, and the grop-ing in the kitchen with the girl completely naked in his arms. And when he had finished with her, he dispatched her through the back door. Not just a paedophile, but an ungrateful one at that.

When Lawrence Gross developed his film and showed it to the Chief, the dissident was summoned to explain himself. In an inquisitorial atmosphere heavy with subterfuge and threats, he protested his innocence. He recounted the truth, which sounded more ridiculous than a lie. He was promised that nothing would come of it if he did what he knew he had to do as an honourable Justice Party Councillor. Head-in-the-Clouds could make no contribution to the matter, for she had withdrawn into a world of greater isolation and silence than ever before. Aside from her, there was only one other person who truly knew what happened that night, and there were two who thought they knew. The dissident lost his nerve at the mention of the fate of child-molesters in prison. The Chief held on to the evidence just in case, and Head-in-the-Clouds was finally admitted to an asylum, having spoken the last words of her life to Manfred Talbot.

Missus Brophy called everyone to her house after receiving the news that the flyover was back on again. She read a note written by Cathal Callaghan in which he expressed his intention to vote in favour of the plan this time. He explained the reason for his change of heart as resulting from the design-change incorporated in the new plan (the flyover was to be two feet higher than the original). He continued by urging us to see the benefits that would accrue to the populace when the new construction was completed. Twenty minutes off a journey to the airport, quicker access for ambulances, a decrease in road accidents. But we

were not satisfied that it should go ahead. The television crews returned and interviewed my grandfather, who told them of all the times we had gathered
in his front garden at midday in the brilliant sun. This
would be impossible when the flyover was built
because it would block the heat.

We lobbied the councillors as they sat to decide. The
dissident slipped in the back door and at half past ten
the news came that they had voted in favour by a
majority of two. The indignity of being seen to back
down on the flimsy grounds of the additional two feet
was a more attractive proposition for Cathal Callaghan than the prospect of going to prison on a charge of
sexual encounters with a minor.

So we could only watch as the pillars went up and
the road was laid across them. I stood with my grandfather in his garden one day and we watched the
progress. He said to me that if the episode proved
anything, it was that even the gorgeous could be got
at. Then he said, 'I suppose Callaghan couldn't have
his cake and eat it.' I was finally beginning to decipher
the confectionery riddle. It was, perhaps, unfair that
the name of Cathal Callaghan became infamous to us.
He was an innocent victim of the crazed mind of a
juvenile day-dreamer, technical advances in photog-
raphy, a crooked politician, and most of all his own
willingness to take the chicane instead of the straight
road. He had endowed himself with the ability to play
God. He had given himself the power to prevent or
allow the reshaping of the landscape. When he raised
his hand in favour of the new construction, he voted
to stop the sun shining on a piece of ground where it
had shone since the beginning of time. He became a

changer of the earth. The man who altered the midday temperature in my grandfather's garden.

All of this is by way of explaining how it was that poor Rory Brophy could come to stand on the flyover which his mother had tried so desperately to stop, the flyover from which he jumped and landed on his back on a mound of satsumas. It was all a bit ironic. He had grown up in a landscape he did not like which was then intended as the method of his exodus, his ally in death. Yet he had not used it properly and it had gone wrong. He now lay on his back with his hands behind his head and no idea of where he was going. He would later claim that the truck of satsumas was a vehicle from God. Of all the moments it could have passed beneath the flyover, it chose the same moment he had done to jump off. The mathematical permutations of the chain of events that led to this particular truck being where it was when it was were so phantasmagorical that God Himself must have planned it. He short-circuited all the mathematics and put the truck beneath the tumbling sixteen-year-old boy because he did not believe that Rory Brophy should die just yet. He had plans for our spiderman.

If cats have nine lives and deaths, then the rabbits Missus Brophy bought had two. In her years of culinary non-experimentation, she had wiped out more rabbits than the three myxomatosis campaigns launched by the state-governments in Krol, Westerhaven and Laga combined. Her rabbits died when the farmers blew their heads off in the fields, and then they died a second and more humiliating death in the dull and tasteless stews that Missus Brophy concocted around them in her big saucepan. There is something noble, almost heroic, about a rabbit losing its fight for life against the odds of a farmer with a gun in his hands. But there was no posthumous glory for the creatures that ended up in one of Missus Brophy's ensembles. At least salmon or lobster or beef went to meet their maker having been savoured with joy by the taste-buds of men. But Missus Brophy's humble rabbits were never endowed with such culinary mystique. They brought water to no mouths. Eating them was a non-event. 'I hope it's male rabbits you cook,' Softy Mullen Senior said to her one day. 'Why?' said Missus Brophy. 'Because that way you keep the population down. It's like me, I've three sons so I've only to worry about three mickies getting into trouble. If I'd three daughters I'd have to worry about thousands of them.'

Gender unknown to me, Missus Brophy's dead rabbit lay in the big saucepan accompanied by a few carrots and onions. Rory's younger sister sat at the table eating her own dinner and giggling to herself as her mother threatened to do dreadful things to Rory's ear for being so late for his meal. (She was only to aware that Rory's physique did not give him much leeway when it came to missing meals. As reserves of fat went, Rory's bucket was empty.) The prospect of being around to see her brother take a hiding thrilled Rory's sister to the end of her pigtails, especially because he had so often woken her up in the mornings by planting his backside on her sleeping head and farting for all he was worth. So she ate as slowly as she could, quarter-filling her spoon and nibbling at the bones of the dead animal. She then astonished her

26

mother by asking for more, perhaps the first time anyone had ever asked for a second helping of Missus Brophy's rabbit thingy. Then the process began all over again, a quarter-filled spoon and mouse-like nibbling at the meat, and all the time Rory's ears were in increasing peril, but there was still no sign of the young man and the rabbit got colder and colder.

Rory's sister extended her mealtime as long as was humanly possible. She would have liked to have sat and watched the dawn farter get his ears boxed, but that was not worth a third helping of her mother's stew. When her father came home at nine o'clock there was still no sign of the matchstick man. Mister Brophy was tired after a ten-hour shift as conductor on the number 33 bus. Ten hours of screaming children and passengers with handfuls of coins. Ten hours of pushing past fat men standing in the aisles and reading newspapers despite the signs forbidding it. He must have walked ten miles that day, and under very difficult circumstances. After all that, he had come home to what was left of his family.

The three of them set off down the street knocking on every door to enquire if anyone had seen Rory. There had been no sightings. Missus Brophy was adamant that the police should be called to investigate. She thought he might have been abducted by a child-molester, or captured by men in the business of exporting white boys to the Middle East as gigolos. These were dangerous times, she was convinced, and the police must be alerted. Mister Brophy was less alarmed. He was tired and his reflexes were not what they should have been. Indeed he was slightly amused by the whole thing. In fact it would not be mistaken to say that he was proud that his son should

27

have followed the example of more adventurous boys and run away. What a splendidly risky thing for a boy to do, he thought to himself as he reassured his wife that he was also overcome with worry. However, he was of the opinion that it was too early to call in the law. There was little the police could do, with only two of them stationed in the local barracks – two who between them couldn't find an elephant on a bus, never mind a boy on the streets at night. So it was decided to wait until dawn. We all went to bed wondering where Rory had gone.

It is easy for me to say this now, I mean in the light of what did unfold, but I am positive I had a feeling during the night that his life had taken an irreversible turn. That he would never again eat his mother's food in the evenings and that he had lived on Cavendish Road for the last time. Wherever he was, I say again that I felt he would never be back. Of that I am sure I was sure. What I did not know was whether he was alive or dead.

After a sleepless night in their house, the Brophys began their first day without Rory since the morning before he was born. Mister Brophy went to the Happy Supermarket ('The More You Spend, The Happier You Get') to make a phone call to the bus depot to say that he would not be coming to work that day as he had to go and find his missing son. He asked Georgie Dunwoody, his driver on the number 33, to tell all the drivers to bless themselves as they passed the statue of Mary of Monk in the depot courtyard on their way out, and to keep their eyes peeled for his boy during the day. 'How will we know him if we see him?' asked Georgie Dunwoody. 'You'll know him,' said Mister Brophy, 'he looks like a skeleton on hunger strike.'

When he had finished that call, Mister Brophy telephoned the police station to report a missing person. Within the hour the officious-looking Inspector Ivor Throckmorton arrived and announced that, although it was still too early to officially declare Rory missing, there were three essentials to successfully solving a case of this nature: a good nose, good intelligence, and good luck. His authoritative manner brought some relief to the people gathered in Missus Brophy's front room. The Inspector knew when he was in the company of an audience which was in awe of his knowledge of his job, and to impress them even more he quoted the number of several articles of the Police Code which empowered him to declare Rory missing forty-eight hours after the last sighting of him by a third party. When he had run out of quotes which he could safely recite without humming and hawing, the Inspector took some details of Rory's appearance (giving an occasional snigger) and the boy's past record as far as running away was concerned. He told everyone that he would keep an eye out for him on his rounds and to call him the next day if Rory had not returned.

When the morning came the Inspector was called again and informed that there had been no sighting of Rory Brophy. 'Very well,' he said, 'at three o'clock this afternoon I will sign the necessary papers and offer you police time and effort in this matter.' At five minutes to three two days previous, old Malachy Dunion had been sitting in front of his radio listening to 'There's Life in You Yet', in which the elderly were given hints on how to make several meals out of the same banana and organising do-it-yourself holidays in their own homes. While sitting there, Malachy Dunion had seen Rory pass in front of his window.

Now, at just before three o'clock, Inspector Throckmorton was in the police station sitting in front of the
enormous typewriter filling out form T27. It was official – Rory Brophy was missing.

Mister and Missus Brophy sat beside the Inspector
as he found the right keys on his machine. When he
had finished he sat back and admired his work.
'There,' he said, tearing the sheet out of the typewriter, 'that's done now.' Rory's parents sat and
looked at him in silence. It was as if they expected that
by correctly filling out the form the Inspector could
produce their son from the next room. Mister Brophy
had told his wife all day that by three o'clock the
police would be involved and that everything would
be fine then. Now they were involved, but the Inspector seemed more intent on admiring the bureaucracy
than finding the boy. It was an anti-climax for them.
The three sat and looked at each other for a few
moments and then the Inspector called to his charge,
the aptly named Officer Bridge, to get his finger out of
his nose and fetch Wino the labrador.

We all joined the search, forming small parties of
three and four and dividing up the area. It took us
three days to look everywhere. Then the Inspector
widened the search. He notified other stations and the
last picture taken of Rory – on the day before we went
back to school the previous summer – was posted in
shopfront windows with the words 'Have you seen
this boy?' printed in bold letters above it. But nobody
seemed to have seen him. Two hundred people took
part in the search led by the officious Inspector of
Police and his nose-picking subordinate, complete
with randy labrador. Wino spent more time sniffing
after sex than he did after Rory. He caused numerous

false alarms by barking furiously and dragging his handler after him, the Officer shouting, 'I think we've got something, I think we've got something . . . Go on, Wino, take me to him.' But Wino would have sniffed nothing more than a chance of a good time with one of the local bitches and the search failed to produce a single clue.

Inspector Throckmorton decided it was time to leave aside the 'good nose' part of his procedural trinity and try to gather some 'good intelligence'. He spoke to Malachy Dunion. 'All I could see of him was his head,' said Malachy Dunion. 'I was sitting in my chair waiting for the radio programme to begin, because there was an item on how to make lamp-shades out of old socks. But from where I was all I could see was the boy's head above the wall.' 'I see,' said the Inspector. 'Then can you tell me how his head looked. Was it a worried head? Did he make any gestures with it or intimate anything? Did he give any clues as to where he was going? What did that head tell you?' With such lines of questioning, the Inspector was making little advance in his drive to collect useful intelligence.

As Rory's best friend, he questioned me about his recent behaviour. Embarking on a résumé of police psychology, he informed me of the tendency for people to display radical changes in behaviour in the period leading up to a disappearance or suicide. There was often a frantic search for identity, which some-times took a religious form. A sudden interest in God. An unprecedented disposition to receive the sacra-ments with great regularity. The purchasing of reli-gious artefacts and literature. Perhaps an effort to inculcate in their peers a desire to follow the same

31

lifestyle. 'Did Rory Brophy display any of these traits recently?' Inspector Throckmorton asked me. 'No, Sir,' was all I could say. 'I see. Well, thank you. You can go now.'

The fact that we did not find Rory in those early days, having looked in all the undergrowth, behind the big warehouses and down the smelly lanes that no one ever went into, convinced me that he was still alive and that he had not met some terrible end. I began to believe that he had simply gone away. Again, it is easy for me to say this with the benefit of hindsight, but I am certain that my recollection of the way I felt at that time is correct. If he had met with an accident in the area, then we would surely have found him alive or dead during the search. I was sure that he had not been the victim of some pervert in a car with a bag of sweets. Without being too cruel to him, Rory was not the ideal subject for such a person. There were far better-looking children around. Although the possibility could not be completely discounted, any motorist with sweets on his dashboard and malice on his mind would have taken one look at Rory and guessed that if offered one from the packet, the boy would have taken the lot as he looked to have never been fed.

The days became weeks became months and there was still no sign of Rory Brophy. The children began to drift back on to the streets, having been kept indoors in the period after the disappearance in an atmosphere of unease at the likely presence of a child-snatcher in our midst. Inspector Throckmorton's intelligence operation had come to nothing and he was forced to admit that all we could do was hope and pray that we got lucky (the final part of his trinity and the last refuge of the baffled policeman). It was only as these weeks and months went by that I began to miss Rory. In the early days the excitement had concentrated our minds and given us the feeling that we were doing something for him. Now that we had searched everywhere three or four times and come to the conclusion that it was pointless to continue, only now did we get to sit on our own and contemplate what had actually happened: that one of ours had simply disappeared, gone, vanished.

As to be expected, it was Rory's parents who suffered the most – in particular his mother, who changed completely. Where once she had been an organiser of people, now she organised nothing. The City Council could have sent her a letter informing her of plans to build an airport in her bathroom, and she would have cared nothing of it. (To every dark cloud there is a silver lining. The rabbits of the nation could be eternally grateful to Rory, for his mother lost all interest in cooking them.) His father went back to his bus. During his long days he was constantly faced with the spectacle of fathers with their sons. He grew sensitive to how badly some of them treated their offspring. How easily they became irritated by simple things like very little children standing up to look out of the windows instead of sitting down. So many fathers ordering their sons to be seated. As if it makes any difference, Mister Brophy would think to himself. If the child wants to stand up then let it; the world will still go around tomorrow.

I learnt at a later stage that the Brophy household lived a curious existence in the absence of Rory. When the table was set, it was set for four. His bedroom was kept in a state of readiness for his return. The bed was made and the clothes were changed, washed and aired along with the clothes from the other beds. Most tragic of all was their first Christmas without him. They debated whether they should buy him presents, but decided against it. A woman by the name of Maude Tennison was the mother of a large family of idiots. It appeared to me that her family had been allotted a fixed quota of brains, so that with each new arrival – and there were many of those – the Tennisons already around grew more stupid. This woman swore on the grave of her mother that she saw Missus Brophy buying half a dozen *Calypso Annuals For Boys* (Rory's favourite) in the book department of Giltrap & Scales. I have always doubted the truth of this report, seeing as it would have meant that the Mother of Morons was in the book department at the time. There was no conceivable reason for her to be in there, given that none of the Tennisons could read.

The Brophys rejected the advice of the representatives of church and state who visited them during those times. Father Sebastian prayed with them in their front room, and told them that they must face the possibility of not seeing their son again. The social worker gave them the names of people who had suffered similar tragedies so that they could speak to them and find some kindred succour. The civil servant from the Department of the Administration brought the official condolences of the state, but also the difficult news that Rory would not receive a voting card on the occasion of his eighteenth birthday because he no longer existed.

I regarded my own impending eighteenth birthday with more than a little horror. 'What are you going to do for it?' people kept asking me. 'It's your eighteenth, you will be able to vote.' Others seemed to watch the days tick by with more interest than I did; and all would add the bit about being able to vote. It was as if reaching this stage in my life released some innate biological capacity which enabled me to mark a ballot paper. Just as I grew my first tooth when I was six months old, and became pubescent when I was twelve, I would be able to vote when I was eighteen. 'Go down and vote those Justice bastards out,' was my grandfather's advice. Ever since the building of the flyover he had abbreviated the party's name to 'those Justice bastards'.

'Nothing, really,' I would answer to questions about my plans for a celebration. 'I have nothing planned.' People looked at me with surprise and disappointment when I told them this. Sometimes they would answer with a big puff of air blown from their mouths, indicating that they didn't believe me and saying, 'Oh! But you are young.' This annoyed me. I was perfectly aware that I was young in relation to the overall age of the population, but what was the relevance of this to the question of having a party? What was it about being young that made people think you instinctively wanted to throw parties at every available opportunity? It was not that a lot of young people did not like the idea, but it seemed that, in many people's eyes, being young and throwing parties was akin to being a woman and having babies – they were the only kind of people who could have them. When I told questioners that I was not interested in a party, nor in making a big occasion of my electoral enfranchisement, they regarded me in the way that people do a woman after a hysterectomy.

It was not a mental problem they saw, but a private, physical one which was best not discussed in public.

Some of them believed that I was not a 'full' person, capable of performing all the tasks for which I was sent here. When the morning of my birthday arrived I received grudging congratulations. I was sent a number of cards by post – we had a tradition of posting each other cards and not just handing them over on the day, probably because it smacked of going to a little effort. As well as the cards, I received my voting certificate and another envelope with my name typed on it and, in the top left-hand corner, the words 'Private and Confidential'. This unexpected addition to my mail that day brought the total to six letters – a record which has yet to be broken.

I opened the envelopes that I knew contained my cards: one each from my mother, father, grandfather and Missus Brophy. My voting card was in a brown envelope without a stamp and included the instruction that I was to take it with me whenever I went to vote and keep it in a safe place at all other times. All of these I had expected, so my surprise was faked. But it was the sixth envelope, the white one with 'Private and Confidential' written on it, which attracted my attention. Who in the world would have something of such privacy to write to me about? I hid the letter in my shirt pocket and ate my breakfast to the mutterings of my mother telling me that she still thought it would have been a good idea for me to have had a party. I was eating toast and definitely know that there was marmalade on it. I also know for sure that it was my first slice. I remember this because it was while eating it that it struck me that I had not looked at the postmark on the letter. More than likely it had been posted in the city somewhere, but there was always a chance that it came from outside.

I waited until my mother had her back to me, pouring water into a kettle of tea, and then I slipped my hand into my shirt pocket and pulled the envelope up slightly. Straining my eyes down as far as I could and digging my chin into the bottom of my neck, I caught sight of the postmark and it was the most invigorating word I had ever seen. I was at the epicentre of an earthquake, the pinnacle of an orgasm (imaginary as I was still a virgin at the time). I was at time zero, the Gates of Heaven, falling over Niagara. I was Galileo when he first saw the rings of Saturn. I pushed the envelope back down into my pocket and continued eating with unnecessary ferocity. Then, feeling the need to duplicate the discovery, I checked again. I was right. My eyes were playing no tricks – the postmark clearly read 'Stockholm'. This is why I remembered the details of what I was eating, just as people recall what they were doing when Kennedy was assassinated. When I had finished eating I locked myself into my bedroom to read my letter, all the way from Stockholm. There was an unpronounceable address in the top right-hand corner but wherever in Stockholm it came from, the sender lived at number 10. It was a long letter too, five and a half pages, typed, like the address on the envelope. Before reading it, I looked at the name on the bottom. It too was typed and there was no signature. Just one typed word: 'Rosbert'.

2   *A Letter for Me*

The scene in the class-room was one of absolute chaos. There had been a spate of calamities that morning, but everyone had apparently taken them in their stride. Schoolrooms have never been immune to calamities, and as far as they are concerned each incident stands on its own, unconnected to the calamity before or the one after. I felt differently as I was going through a stage when I believed I was being contacted by the supernatural. This had begun three weeks before The Morning of Consecutive Calamities, when Mister Roberto Poidevan, literature teacher *extraordinaire* and possessor of a treasure trove of personal anecdotes, was telling us about the death of his mother. He was very easily side-tracked into telling stories and we had become very adept at steering him away from the work of the Romantics, or some other movement of complete irrelevance to us, and towards telling us stories from his past. He had a wonderful collection from his days in Africa, for instance his narrow escape from death when a green mamba slid into his car while he was parked by a river at midday saying the Angelus. He exuded special pride when telling us of how he had converted the women of a small village to the brassière. We found this a tale of extraordinary self-denial, and after he related it some of the students began to consider whether the missionary life might be for them. Their deliberations centred not on doubts about receiving a vocation, but on whether there were still parts of the Third World where women went without clothes. Mister Poidevan's story about the brassière suggested that there might be, but also that such places were becoming scarce and that Softy Mullen's paradise of a life surrounded by 'big black bouncy ones' was daily becoming less and less attainable.

It was the story of the death of Mister Poidevan's mother that began what I thought was my period of contact with the other side. He told us of how he had been sitting at home in the evening eating a meal when he received a call from the hospital saying that his mother had taken a very bad turn and that he should come at once. She had been in the hospital for quite some time and there was nothing that could be done for her. Mister Poidevan had no car, so he jumped on a bus which left him half a mile from the hospital. Walking up a tree-lined avenue he noticed a woman advancing quickly behind him. As she passed him, and he was walking quickly himself, he was seized by the urge to ask her for the time, despite having a watch of his own. The woman (who apparently thought she was about to be beaten and robbed on a quiet tree-lined avenue, with no one about to help her) was so relieved at the question that she replied in a very happy voice, 'Seven thirty-five precisely, Sir, and isn't it a beautiful evening?' Mister Poidevan's mother was dead when he reached the hospital minutes later and the doctor's report stated that she died at seven thirty-five p.m.

This story was to have a profound effect on me because it was told by a man I believed to be incapable of telling a lie. The logic of its thus incontrovertible truth was that we must be capable of receiving signals from the dying or the dead which make us do things which are irrational. What troubled me was the intent behind such communication. During his story, Mister Poidevan told us that he had loved his mother very much and that she had been a woman of great intelligence and generosity, especially towards her children. Yet at the very moment she passed away (and I must totally exclude the possibility of coincidence as the statistical chances of it being so are so infinitesimal as to be irrelevant), she, or an agent acting on her behalf, made some contact with her son which made him behave in an irrational way. Again, I was assuming that her death and his enquiring the time were connected by some supernatural system of communication. If this was the case and the initiative came from her, then there were two possible reasons why she should make him do such a thing. On the positive side, there was the possibility that this was the only way she could notify him of her death. By making him ask a total stranger the time, despite having a watch on his wrist, she could have been signalling her death to him in a most memorable way. A remarkable end to a very close friendship. However, impelled by a mistrust I had of the dead as knowing something we did not, I dwelt longer on the other, more sinister possibility. Could it have been that, at the moment of her transition into the far side, and catching a glimpse of what it was like, she had pulled the strings of Mister

Poidevan and sent him off puppet-like to do something stupid? This story of absurd behaviour at the point of demise confirmed a suspicion I had been entertaining that good people were changed completely by death and became instantly wicked. At that stage my theory had not widened to embrace the effect of death on those who had committed evil during their lives. I was not certain that death was a lens which inverted everything, just that good became evil. Since the fate of evil remained a matter for conjecture, I had not yet befriended any thugs in the hope that they might do me favours when they passed on.

It was during the development of this theory that I heard the story of Mister Poidevan's mother, and my nights became times of endless fear. I dreaded the onset of darkness and, when I did go to bed, I would lie awake for hours in fear of the prospect of Missus Poidevan or some other dead person making contact with me. After six days of this I was physically very weak and my mother told me that I should see a doctor because of my anaemic complexion. I thanked her for her concern and reassured her that it was nothing more than exam nerves, and even received some sympathy for this lie. But on the seventh night after hearing Mister Poidevan's story (anniversaries are a big thing with the dead), a week to the day, I lay on my bed in total darkness and received my first signal – three knocks on the cavity wall that divided my bedroom from the toilet. They had found me and they were in the wall. (To the day I left that house I never deliberately knocked against the cavity wall. Even after the crisis had passed, I would still be careful about touching it in case they were still in there, like jellyfish abandoned on a beach by a retreating tide.

But that is later.) I lay in a state of paralysis. The knocking stopped. This was my first contact, the first of three – again, a loaded number.

For the moment, my fear was confined to the night and my days were given over to reflection and analysis. I was trying to rationalise the visitation, as this seemed the best way to proceed. Ignoring it was out of the question. I studied the faces of other students for signs of similar disorientation. Perhaps they were being affected too. Perhaps it was part of ageing, like teething and pubic hair and being able to vote at eighteen. But I saw no signs of kindred spirits (maybe an unwise choice of words). I came to the conclusion that I was alone in this and that I had been singled out as a medium. It was all getting too much for me.

There are two kinds of shock: those you can see coming and those you can't. Mister Hitchcock was a great believer in the former. He made it clear to you that something awful was about to happen. The skill of the audience was in guessing when it would happen so they could prepare themselves. The three knocks on the cavity wall were of this variety. I was expecting something and felt that it would occur at night, but I did not know which night and what form the event would take. My second contact shook me to the balls of my feet, and proved Mister Hitchcock right to believe that advance warning is no panacea at all. It happened, I estimate, two weeks after the cavity wall incident, though not exactly two weeks after because it was a Sunday. My parents had gone to the country to visit an aunt who had moved to an isolated cottage up some mountain or other. Assuming they would be back by nightfall, I excused myself from the drudgery of the visit by spinning an extraordinarily complex lie about an appointment I had with Rory Brophy to visit an exhibition in the Hall of the Brilliance of Our Ancestors, because Rory was considering working with precious metals when he left school. The lie began quite bumblingly, but then just exited my mouth like a magician's endless string of handkerchiefs. It was only after I had finished that my father explained that they would not be coming back that night. After the effort I had put into my lie, I couldn't change my mind without them becoming suspicious of my story or thinking I was afraid to spend the night alone in the house. They would, of course, have been right on both counts.

When they had gone it was still afternoon and there were games being played on the street. People were tending their gardens or standing at their gates talking to each other. The whole world was happy bar one, and I sat on the big sofa in the front room thinking that this would be the first night I had ever spent alone in the house, and this at a time when I was being contacted from the other side. I felt that music might help, so I crossed the room and put on a record. I sat on the floor with a cushion beneath me, leaning back against the leg of the sofa. There was a saxophone playing and someone outside on the street shouted 'Mary!' As the sax solo came to an end Mary answered 'What!' and just as she did so, the door of the room pushed open. I looked at it. It was half open. I knew I was dreaming a bit, not concentrating on the door. But then it was the door opening which had broken my concentration. There was a carpet on the floor of the room and so some force had to be applied to the door to open it. It could not just have slipped off the latch. I sat numb on the cushion looking at it. When I was able to move, I stood up and craned my neck to see if there was anyone on the other side. I called to Rory thinking it might be a prank, but there was no answer. I raced into the hallway, up the stairs and into every room. There was nobody else in the house, at least none that were visible. Ill with fear, I ran into the garden where the daylight offered some comfort. I went to sleep that night at about four a.m. with all the lights on and the radio up loud. When I woke up at seven I was lying on the sofa, very cold and tired. It was daylight, so I went upstairs and got into bed.

It was during the following week that they sent me The Morning of Consecutive Calamities. It began as I walked the few hundred yards to school and arrived at the gate to find Samuel Kick standing at it with someone else I did not recognise. Samuel Kick was three years older than me and I had some respect for him because he never joined the others when they dumped the youngsters in the long-jump pit and pushed sand down their trousers. As I passed them, this unknown person stood out in front of me and demanded all my money. I looked to Samuel Kick to intervene. He knew me and surely would tell this shit-dressed-up to let me pass. But Samuel Kick just looked away and left me to be burgled. When I reached the class-room I was red with anger. Robbed I had been. Divested of my paltry wealth at the gates. 'A shit dressed up,' I murmured, 'A shit with a shirt on.'

My school-bag in those days was a source of great pride to me. I had been given it by my neighbour Harold Orwell, who was a civil servant of no great seniority except in his own mind. He would stand at the bus-stop in the morning, very erect with his head held back and a big serious face at the front of it. If time given to thinking about the problems of the world was a decisive factor in solving them, then Harold Orwell could have saved us all. But he had little chance of doing so as the most pressing difficulty which crossed his desk at the Ministry of Justice was the equitable sharing of the urine-sampling of drunken drivers amongst the city's doctors, who would be up in arms if they did not get their fair share of piss. Given the job he held it seemed extraneous to requirements, but Harold Orwell could not go to work without his bulging briefcase, which stood beside him like an obedient labrador at the bus-stop every morning. Much as we joked about his briefcase, I confess to being absolutely delighted when I inherited it. He passed it over the back hedge to me one day. 'Why?' I asked him. 'Because I've got a bigger one,' he said. It was black leather with boards on both sides to stiffen it, and had a leather strap that flapped across the top and locked it. 'A shit with trousers,' I said, sitting down and placing my case on the ground beside me.

I continued this for a short while until disturbed by a scuffle which broke out behind me. It was Softy Mullen and Davy Dunstable, the two biggest people in the room. Davy Dunstable had feet the size of doors yet he still managed to fall over in my direction, bringing Softy Mullen with him, the two of them crashing down on top of my case, which had been in my possession only three weeks. A combined weight of over twenty stone flattened it and it lay like a dead plaice with both sides snapped and big tears along the stitching at both ends.

The third calamity of the morning involved blood. Again it was a scuffle, this time Brinsley Bates and Bernard Troy in a mock sumo fight. As Bates lunged forward, his opponent simply stepped out of the way, sending Bates's head through a window, tearing half his forehead off. Such a series of calamities within the space of a couple of hours had me thinking that *they* had started a campaign of attrition against me in which I would be worn down like a limestone rock. It was then that Mister Poidevan entered. I was growing very tired of him, as he was responsible for much of my paranoia at that time. True to form, it was not long before he had again been side-tracked, this time to the story of Osbert Selkirk, the notorious mass murderer of the early part of the century.

Osbert Selkirk was a man who murdered his wife and six children by mixing anti-rust treatment in their rhubarb. He then fed their bodies to his pigeons who grew too fat to race any more, so he mixed glass in their water and fed them to his cats. The case so enraged the public that huge crowds gathered outside the court-house every day of his trial to scream for punishment. When he was found guilty, the prison authorities notified the judge that they could not guarantee his safety, so he was sentenced to death for his own protection. But the sentence was never carried out. Osbert Selkirk was consumed by the most horrible nightmares which had him screaming throughout the hours of darkness. Each night he would be tormented by a different member of his family and he would call to each one for forgiveness. On Saturday nights it was the turn of Rebecca, his youngest child, who was only seven when she ate one plate of rhubarb too many. She seemed to torment him the most and became a favourite with the other prisoners. His cries could be heard on the streets outside the prison and many people made it a regular part of their evening entertainment. The deck-chair merchants from the beaches at Yivon would bring their equipment up to the prison on Saturday evenings after dusk and hire them out to the crowds. 'Go get him, Rebecca,' people would shout and the crowd would often break into a three-syllabled chant, 'Rebec-ca, Re-bec-ca', clapping their hands in rhythm and bursting into applause whenever he screamed for mercy. 'Death would be too good for this monster,' people would say. 'This is true justice.' Mister Poidevan was a young child at the time and his mother would not allow him to go near the prison at night because she believed the whole thing was barbaric. But one Saturday night he managed to escape from his room and join the huge crowd outside the prison, which was in real carnival mood. A fat man with bad breath told him that he had been going there every Saturday for three months. 'Everyone knows that when the monster dies it will be on Saturday,' said the man. 'That's because Rebecca will take him . . . She's a real angel is Rebecca.' Osbert Selkirk died a few Saturday nights after that and the carnival was at an end. I felt nothing but sympathy for him, as if we were kindred spirits (I must choose my phrases more carefully). The horror of his crime was lost on me. It was of no consequence and I forgave him. In the last months of his life he had been subjected to the most terrible torment possible. I tried to imagine what it was like for him and my own experiences paled into insignificance in comparison.

Osbert Selkirk became a kind of martyr to me and I tried to defend him as we walked home on that Morning of Consecutive Calamities. There were four or five of us, I can't remember exactly, but I know that

Rory Brophy was one of them. The others were saying that they would have loved to have been outside the prison on the nights of his torment. One of them suggested telephoning the national radio station to enquire if there was a recording available. I did my best for him, but the jury was packed against me. Rory Brophy admitted to hating his sister, but the thought of putting anti-rust treatment in her rhubarb and feeding her to the pigeons – well, this was unimaginable. 'But nobody deserves to go the way he did,' I protested. 'They should have hung him and got it over with. And all those crowds outside the prison – it shouldn't have been allowed. The police should have sent them home.' But this was as far as I could go. Any stronger defence would have left me open to being marked as a sympathiser, an apologist for infanticide. No one would ever eat my cooking.

I felt a desperate need to tell someone what was happening to me. It had to be someone who would understand and who would believe me, even though what I was saying sounded incredible. My decision was to tell someone who had themselves been the subject of torment in the past and I could think of no one else who had suffered so much as Rory Brophy. His physique had been his cross in life. The matchstick man would not laugh at me. He would be honoured that someone was actually coming to him with a problem, so I told Rory Brophy.

I told Rory Brophy that very evening in the front room of my house. I had resolved to reveal all so I took him upstairs and showed him the cavity wall (being careful not to touch it). I sat down on the cushion in the front room and demonstrated how the door had opened by itself. I showed him my bleary eyes from lack of sleep and explained that this was why I had attempted to defend Osbert Selkirk. It was nothing to do with agreeing with his actions. I was sure his wife and children had been wonderful people who had not deserved such a fate. It was just that both Osbert Selkirk and I had had similar experiences – we had both been contacted from the other side.

Rory listened attentively to everything I said before taking a deep breath and pronouncing me 'crazy'. To add insult, as he was leaving the room he quickly pushed the door open and stuck his skinny head back in and went 'Boooooo!' I was furious with him. He of all people should have understood what it was like to be in trouble and feel down and worried. Perhaps all of the punishment he had taken had numbed his senses and he had gotten tough to avoid being hurt.

Whatever the reason, he had shown no under-standing of my predicament and in the days that followed he began to call me 'Osbert'. In a pathetic attempt to get back at him with a devastatingly witty reply, I began to call him 'Rosbert' (taking the first two letters of his name). I admit this was a stunningly inept retort, but it was the best I could do. To give due credit to him, I believe he did not tell anyone of our conversation, for no one else ever mentioned it to me.

I have never been able to explain my experiences. I am as sure today as I was then that they did occur. They continue to occupy my thoughts and influence my thinking on the afterlife, but the panic has passed now. Perhaps there is truth to my theory of death being a lens which inverts personalities, and perhaps my defence of Osbert Selkirk won favour with him. The mass murderer in life may have become my guardian angel, for I have had no more experiences such as those. In any case, this is by way of explaining the origin of the name 'Rosbert' that was written at the bottom of my letter from Stockholm. Only two people knew of this name and I was one of them. As far as the state was concerned, it would have been a contact from the dead, for they had eventually declared him so. But it was very much a contact from the living. After nearly two years of hearing nothing, my suspicions were confirmed. Rory Brophy was alive and he had written me a letter – all the way from Stockholm.

3 *Keeping a Secret*

Rory's letter began by insisting that I must tell no one that I had heard from him. If I was not prepared to do so, then I should read no further and destroy the letter. I wondered if he seriously believed that I would burn it without reading it, knowing the turmoil that would have followed his disappearance. To believe that I would destroy such crucial evidence because I thought I could not keep my mouth shut was at worst enormously naïve and at best displayed a very flattering confidence in my integrity. He even left a couple of blank lines for me to consider his ultimatum. I agreed that I would stay quiet, although the sincerity of this decision was very dubious given my interest in the letter. (In such circumstances the difficulty in fulfilling the promise is always furthest from your mind.) So by reading on I was drawing myself into this great mystery and committing myself to a difficult future.

What I knew would be most difficult was facing his parents again. They had not recovered from their loss and I doubted that they ever would, at least not until they knew what had happened to him. I remembered my mother's words on the comfort she received from going to the box-room in my grandfather's house where she had been born. It was all about having somewhere to go, a special, sacred place. Like when people went to tend graves. It was just somewhere to visit and fuss over. But Rory's mother and father had no such place. This was why grieving had been so difficult for them. In a way I was annoyed with Rory for doing such a thing to them, because they were good people. His mother was the world's worst cook, but she was a good woman. And his father, who spent his days listening to crying babies and pushing his way past stubborn passengers on his bus, he deserved more than this. Could I ever face them again and not tell them what I knew? Could I stand and watch their hearts break slowly through the years when I had the power to save them with just a few words? Such a simple thing it would have been, if integrity had not been an issue. These were the things that I should have but did not consider as I read on. That I was breaking the law by concealing evidence did not occur to me either. What Inspector Throckmorton would have given for this new evidence! What good intelligence this would have been for him.

After the two-line gap left for me to consider his proposal, Rory continued by telling me the manner of his disappearance. I had thought that he had just decided to leave – it had never crossed my mind that his departure was a failed attempt to kill himself. His decision to walk on to the flyover and throw himself from it had been reached in a surprisingly short space of time. He wrote of the ease with which he had made it. No prolonged debate, just a decision made within a few minutes and with a clear head. 'Our bodies and our brains are our tickets to success,' he went on. He thought of the younger children on the street, the young girls who were only four and five but already had such innate beauty. You could tell that it was only a matter of time before that beauty began to develop into something wonderful. They were just like flower seeds: once you put them in the ground the only things they could grow into were flowers. It was just a question of waiting, letting nature take its course, and their beauty would emerge. Their ticket to freedom and success. And the young boys. Weren't they all more popular than he? They had such developed personalities. It was so effortless for them to get on with people and to be liked. He found this particularly upsetting: because he was older, his personality should have been more advanced. It was supposed to be a cumulative process – the older you get, the more adept you become at getting on with people. It was humiliating for him to be upstaged by younger people, and he always felt intimidated by them. It was not only that they badgered him because of his build . . . There was an inner feeling that he had about himself, a feeling of disappointment that he had fallen behind. He had not used the years properly and he could not get them back – they were gone forever. It was this sense of irreparable damage that depressed him so much that he made his attempt to end it all. So he climbed to the highest part of the flyover and waited for a truck to come down the motorway.

When his chosen one did arrive, he timed his jump and leapt into its path, but the wind trapped beneath the flyover tossed his bag of bones about and suspended him for those few seconds before dropping him on his back into the rear of the truck. His eyes still closed, he thought it was all over and that death had a softish landing on a lumpy surface that smelled of oranges. This was Heaven – he was sure he would go there, having been one of life's sufferers. He had not considered whether his senses would still function in the afterlife, but was immediately aware of a smell. 'Just imagine,' he thought to himself, 'Heaven smells of oranges.' (Extraordinary how the mind works.) He could also sense that he was hurtling forward. This was strange, because he distinctly remembered hearing of people who had almost died speak of a sensation of falling backwards. But he was definitely moving forwards. Perhaps he had died facing the wrong direction? At any rate he was certainly hurtling forward in what smelt like a jar of marmalade. He could feel the surface beneath him was soft and consisted of circular objects smaller than tennis balls. He moved his hands on either side and discovered that he could drive them down between these small balls. 'What are these?' he thought to himself. 'Clouds, maybe. That's it, I'm lying on a cloud – clouds smell of oranges too.'

His eyes remained closed – he believed he was only seconds into death. This forward motion he was experiencing would take him quickly to his destination. He had always imagined that the spirit travelled very quickly after death – it had to because the Universe was so vast. He guessed that he must be going at the speed of light, if not faster. This was fantastic. He was delighted with his suicide, a brilliant decision. He was so exhilarated he noticed a developing erection. Maybe that was what Heaven was, just one long eternal orgasm, that magic moment extended a billion times. These were the things he thought of in those few minutes after his attempt to exit the world.

Then the forward motion stopped. He was not at the Gates of Heaven, just a set of traffic lights. And he was not lying on a cloud of orange-smelling balls, but in a truck full of satsumas. When he did finally realise what had happened to him he made no effort to do anything. He just lay on his back, ate some fruit and began to think about himself in a way he had never done before. He mused that strength was as relative as speed, and that in terms of the dominant forces that controlled life and death the physical strength of an individual was immaterial. The only strength that mattered was that which could alter the way people think, an intellectual strength which could enrich or destroy the spirit of men. His own frailty of mind had stemmed from his consciousness of the body it was in, and was thus an illusion. He could sense a spiritual awakening, a realignment of his thoughts, right there as he lay on the satsumas. If his journey was to take him somewhere he had never seen before, then it would be a perfect opportunity to begin again. So he ate more fruit and began to consider the proximity to death he had engineered. It had, in fact, been his featherweight body which had saved him. A heavier one would have dropped straight down and perished. This was fantastic. What an opportunity.

In the hours that followed he was driven to the port at Sion and dumped into a huge ship. It happened very quickly and unexpectedly. His feet were raised up and he slid backwards and downwards, his body overrun by tumbling satsumas. His shouts were drowned out by the hydraulic engine of the truck and the thousands of satsumas falling into the ship. When

57

his fall ended, he found himself buried and had to dig his way up. Thinking of this later, he wondered how he had known which way to dig. But he chose correctly, like the shoot of a germinating seed growing up to the light. He had barely got his head free when a second truck emptied its load on top of him and he had to dig up again. This clamour for life he had to repeat several times before the hull of the ship was full – wherever he was going, they sure did like satsumas. When they had finished loading the fruit the huge doors of the hull were slid shut and he was in complete darkness. He only kept the top half of his head above the level of the fruit so as not to be seen. As further camouflage he built a mound of the fruit up the sides of his face. But now that he was in darkness he climbed free, lay on his back to sleep, and lost track of time.

The hull of the ship was perfectly sealed. There were no cracks through which he could see if it was day or night, so time ceased to be a factor in his life. This was the first occasion since childhood that he was not rushing to be somewhere. His days had always been punctuated by deadlines. Get up in time to eat breakfast. Eat breakfast in time to get to school. Come home from school in time for tea. Finish homework in time for dinner. Be back home in time for bed. Always a deadline and never space for things to take their course. Not until now. Not until he found this fruit time-capsule.

He couldn't say how long he had been lying there – all he knew was that he ate forty satsumas. It ended when the doors of the hold were slid back. Rory reacted like an insect beneath an overturned rock. He quickly dug his way down into the fruit until only the tip of his nose stuck up to let him breathe easily. There was no reaction from above. Nothing happened at all. He guessed he must have been wedged there for half an hour waiting for something to happen, but nothing did. A cramp began to develop in his right leg. He shook it a few times but this gave little relief. Then it hit him very badly. His leg was seized by excruciating pain and he had no alternative but to jump up and lie on his back, grabbing his leg and trying to bend the toes on his right foot back. This eased the pain a little, but meant he was now completely visible. There was still no activity on deck, so he took his chance and ran for it. At the side of the hold he was able to reach up and grab the edge of the opening. His skinny arms weren't very strong but then they had little to lift. He raised himself up until his head was above the level of the deck, but there was no one to be seen. He climbed up and ran for a narrow gangway which led across on to the pier. As he set foot on land, a fat sailor in a vest came out of a cabin shouting at him. He had a cup of tea in one hand and a sandwich in the other. His obscenities sent bits of bread and ham shooting out in an arc around his face. But Rory was away and running.

He ran up somewhere called Djurgards Vagen with the water on his left. He turned on to Strand Vagen where he met a group of people who appeared to be tourists. Afraid that he was being followed, Rory Brophy mingled with the group and followed them up a short street until they went into a café and sat down. They took a number of tables and one of them called to a waiter to bring coffee and scones. Rory took a table next to them from where he could look across at the brochures they were browsing through. One of them was entitled 'Nordic Museum and Royal Armoury, Stockholm'. 'Stockholm,' Rory muttered to himself. 'Jesus, I'm in bloody Denmark.' Then a cup of coffee and two hot scones were placed in front of him by the efficient waiter who had mistaken him for a tourist. These were the first hot things he had eaten in a while and they tasted superb after all the satsumas. He timed his consumption to keep a little ahead of the fastest tourist, a man with glasses and a beige mac. When this man had eaten one scone, Rory had eaten one and a half. When he had eaten one and a half scones, Rory had eaten two. When the tourist had finished his second scone, Rory was gone.

He found this technique a useful way to eat and spent the rest of the day searching out groups of tourists. They were not hard to find. It was summer in Stockholm and the restaurants had tables outside where waiters came to take orders. Rory sat in amongst the tourists as they ate and nobody questioned him. The waiters trusted the tourists completely. There was no suggestion of having to pay for a meal in advance or anything as vulgar as that. So Rory fed himself magnificently and walked away. What he needed next was an overcoat, as Stockholm gets very cool in the evenings. The unquestioned honourability of the tourist was to provide the answer to this problem also. As he went up Skepper Gatan, he began to think like a tourist. 'If I think like one I will be better able to convince others that I am one.' He rationalised that, after all, he was a tourist. His method of arrival had been a little unusual, but it is the tourist's prerogative to select his own mode of transport. He had absolutely no money, but his was an economy holiday. 'A tourist is a visitor and nothing more,' he thought to himself. 'Having money doesn't make you any more a tourist. I come from a different country, I speak a different language, my customs are different. I am as much a tourist as the man with the glasses and the beige mac eating scones in the café.'

Thinking in this way, Rory entered a shop with the avowed intention of stealing a coat. There was a single assistant in the shop, a man in his late thirties. He was a little startled when Rory came in as he was probably the most unusual tourist the assistant had ever seen. Rory said he wished to buy a coat, explaining that he had not realised that Denmark got so cold at this time of year and pointing at a line of coats that ran along one wall of the shop. The assistant was full of politeness when he heard the foreign voice and, speaking in broken English, welcomed Rory to Stockholm. He even went so far as to apologise for the weather. 'This one looks very nice,' said Rory, picking out a beige sheepskin from the rack. But because of his ill-proportioned body, the sleeves reached only to the top of his wrists and the hem to just below his backside, when it should have reached the backs of his knees. 'Perhaps it is a little short for you, Sir,' the attendant begged and, continuing to display this faith in the honesty of tourists, disappeared into the back of the shop insisting that he was sure they had a larger size in stock. Such trust has been the downfall of many an individual and, while he was searching through his storeroom, this particular assistant was added to that list. Rory marched quickly from the scene of his latest crime, the worst-dressed tourist in Stockholm. He looked like a lamp-post with a sheep wrapped around it, but he was delighted with his warm overcoat and

61

his full belly. His attempted suicide was becoming a most enjoyable failure.

It was evening-time by this stage and the sun was almost gone. Now he needed to find somewhere to stay that night. In the Rindo Gatan he heard the sound of brass music being played by middle-aged men and women, some of whom collected money from passers-by. 'Excellent,' Rory thought, 'a charity band and somewhere to stay for the night.' He shed the confident persona of a tourist and drooped his shoulders as only he could. He went up to the group and asked for somewhere to spend the night, and was escorted to the Radmans Gatan, where he entered a shabby building which smelt of soup. 'No thank you, I couldn't eat another thing,' he said to a startled woman serving minestrone. He slept in a bleak room with ten single beds of which his was the furthest from the door. Before he fell asleep, two tramps fought for the bed beside the radiator and one ended up with a bleeding skull. It was while watching this drunken brawl that Rory Brophy lost the spirit of adventure which had lasted from the time he leapt from the flyover. His room was dark and damp and he had only a single blanket to cover himself. He wore his coat in bed because the lady with the minestrone had advised him not to let the others see it or he might have his throat slit during the night by a thief.

It was a surreal time as he watched the fight develop for the radiator. It did not worry him because he was thinking of something completely different, namely all that had happened to him. This was far distant from anything he could ever have imagined would happen to him. He contemplated his rampage of crime. In that one day he had been guilty of more wrongdoings than in the rest of his life. He had been a stowaway, had scones and coffee and a very big meal at other people's expense, and then robbed a coat, which he guessed was quite expensive, from a trusting assistant. He thought of his family. This was the first time he had considered what they must be going through because of him. His poor mother of the dreadful rabbit-stew. His father, who broached new boundaries of patience when dealing with his passengers. His sister, the victim of so many of his flatulent attacks at dawn. Rory Brophy spent much of the night in tears, surrounded by the smells of poverty in a building which had known better days. He was crying for himself and for what had happened to him.

He was wakened by a prodding in his ribs. When he opened his eyes there was a face staring right at him, not a foot away from his own. It was a horrible face and it took Rory a few moments to tell harsh reality from nightmare. He was indeed awake and being gaped at by an old man with very dark skin and a face like the surface of a coconut – hard and hairy. The smell of bad breath filled Rory's nostrils as the man signalled him in a half grunt to get up. In the kitchen downstairs, the woman with the minestrone had become the woman with the porridge. They were fed and then ushered on to the street and the bolt slid shut on the door of the building to exclude them. The old man tried to follow him, but Rory wasn't having any of it. He could never be taken for a tourist with such a companion, so he shooed the man away as you would a dog. But he still followed him. It was only by running quickly that he lost him and could go in search of tourists and some morning coffee and scones.

On the waterfront there was a constant traffic of groups of visitors. They were being ushered along by guides who showed them around the city explaining the various places of historic interest. Rory spotted one group loitering around a café, probably discussing whether to have coffee or not. He approached them quickly and when he got there some of the group had sat down while others remained standing. Rory took a table in the middle of them and a waiter was beside him in an instant. 'Yes, Sir,' said the waiter taking a pen from behind his ear. 'Eh . . . One coffee, two scones,' said Rory. As he ordered he noticed that the group had decided not to stay after all. Those already sitting down gathered their belongings and waddled down the street chatting furiously. Rory was left at a table on his own with no one else near but a fat man with a huge moustache who sat at a table twenty yards away and grinned at Rory in a very unsettling way.

Rory Brophy believed that his cover had been blown and that his day of crime was about to catch up with him. He was sure the group of tourists were in on it. Undercover agents probably, very clever. They had lured him into a trap. The waiter arrived back with the coffee and scones and Rory surmised that he must be involved as well. That Rory had ordered the food and there was no one else to pay for it was as obvious as could be.

He looked across at the man with the moustache who was still smiling back at him. 'A police officer of very high rank,' Rory thought to himself, 'here to supervise the operation.' Making a run for it against such odds was out of the question. 'They would probably shoot me in the back for resisting arrest,' he thought. 'Gunned down like a fugitive.' Rory decided that the scam was up and that his time as an outlaw was at an end. Better to go peacefully than risk injury. He had still not touched the scones which were going cold on the plate and he had only taken a single sip from the coffee. When the waiter came out again, Rory called him over and informed him that he had no money to pay, but the waiter didn't seem to understand. He just nodded his head and said, 'Yes, Sir.' 'No, no . . . You don't understand,' said Rory, 'I have no money, *no money, net muni.*' It was not until he pulled his pockets inside out that the waiter got the message and went mildly berserk, shouting for the police. There were none about, but the fat man with the moustache and the smile jumped from his chair and spoke to the waiter in what Rory presumed was Danish. He then produced some coins from his pocket and presented them to the waiter. The waiter stopped shouting and gestured to Rory to clear off. 'Come with me, my boy,' said the fat man, putting his hand on Rory's shoulder. His accent was familiar and Rory thought it to be from his home town. 'I will show you to your hotel,' said the man.

Rory was taken from the scene by the man, his hand still on Rory's shoulder. 'Ha ha . . . I like that . . . I really like that,' the man was saying. 'Like what?' said Rory. 'I was giving myself up and he starts going lunatic.' 'What do you expect? You give an order and then announce that you have no money to pay. These people are fed up with being robbed by tourists. Last week they caught a Dane trying to walk out without paying for two beers. He protested his innocence, of course, then he put it down to a memory lapse, but they still called the police.' 'How can a Dane be a tourist here?' asked Rory. 'What are you on about, you fool,' said the man. 'This is Stockholm, capital of Sweden. The week before last they almost killed a Frenchman who tried to rob a pair of ladies' gloves from one of the stalls in the market. It was the women who caught him. He was lucky there was a police patrol nearby to save him. I tell you, they have had enough of dishonest tourists. Now, which hotel are you staying in? You can pay me back later.' 'I'm not staying in any hotel,' said Rory. 'I'm a stowaway, I've run away.' 'Jesus, you are a donkey,' said the man stopping and looking Rory up and down. 'Where did you stay last night?' 'Last night was my first night. I stayed in a building with the tramps. But I'm not one . . . My father's a bus conductor.' 'Jesus,' said the man again, 'you are a donkey.'

This was the nature of Rory's introduction to Max Sponge, whose favourite word in the English language was 'donkey'. He applied it with ease to everything. Rainy days were 'donkey' days. When the weather was warm, the heat was 'donkey'. Good-looking women (of which there were many in Stockholm) were 'donkey' women, as were ugly women. There were times when the application of the word was confusing. Max was a fan of show-jumping and always went to see the grand prix tour when it visited the city. These outings became a great source of friendship between him and Rory. They would sit in the main stand and Max would occasionally nudge Rory, drawing his attention to the name of a horse in the programme. 'Do you see this one?' he would say. 'Watch this one, it's an absolute donkey of a horse.'

Rory spent the first few days with Max Sponge. The fat man who said 'donkey' a lot and had rescued him from certain arrest was indeed from Rory's home town. It was because he had recognised Rory's accent that he had intervened. Had Rory been a Spaniard or a German, Max Sponge would have sat where he was and done nothing. His decision to have coffee that morning was another indisputable turning-point in Rory's life – a so-called date with destiny in fact, for at that very time Max Sponge was looking to find someone in Stockholm who could speak perfect English and would be willing to help him test a new business idea he had been formulating for some time. This was the reason he had been smiling at Rory on that morning. It was the smile of a crossword buff who has just deciphered the last clue.

Max Sponge lived on the top floor of a four-storey building near the Rindo Gatan where Rory had spent his first night in Stockholm. The three floors below were occupied by the offices of professional people. The apartment was very neat. Max Sponge was fond of art and there were numerous paintings on the walls. None of them were originals. They were all prints in plastic frames. They would prove a perfect testament to Max Sponge's place in the world. Cheap but nice imitations of great things. Well-intentioned grasps for greatness that never quite made it. 'You know I haven't any money to pay you for anything,' Rory said again to Max, who had bought him a good meal that evening and made up a bed on the floor in front of the fire where Rory could spend the night. 'There are other means of payment than money,' Max replied with a laugh. Rory felt decidedly uncomfortable at this remark and looked at Max Sponge with a mixture of fear and amazement, to which the fat man reacted with another laugh. 'Stop worrying, I'm not one of those donkeys. Now go to sleep, we'll talk in the morning.'

It was the most comfortable night Rory had spent in a while. The wood in the fire burned slowly and gave off a very good heat. It seemed a pity to sleep through it, but Rory dozed off staring into the flames and wondering if he was still the same person he had been the previous week, or if he hadn't really died and been quickly reincarnated.

It was during Rory's third day in Stockholm that Max Sponge explained the full reason for saving Rory from the rabid waiter. He was looking for a tall male with good English and Rory certainly met both requirements. It was a risky venture he had in mind, and the fact that he was indebted to him made it more likely Rory would agree. Max Sponge admitted to earning a living in the entertainment business, the lower end of it. He ran a brothel in the city, which had not been doing too well lately. He spoke of his clients as his raw material and of late there had been a problem with continuity of supply. 'It's all this advertising the Tourist Board is doing abroad,' he complained. 'They're portraying Sweden like it's one giant convalescent home with trees. The only tourists we're getting here now are elderly couples. It has damn near put me out of business.' To overcome this problem, Max Sponge had devised a scheme with Oran Phillips, an old friend of his who had been living in Stockholm for thirty years. Oran Phillips lived for only one thing – soccer. All his topics of conversation at some stage converged on the game. Although he was now sixty, Oran Phillips's love for the game had not diminished an iota. He still coached a team called the Furtwangler Kickers, which was established in 1954 by the newly redundant workers of the High Brow Spectacle Frame Manufacturing Company of Stockholm. Since its inception, the club had recruited only three new players, so the average age was forty-eight. This statistic, along with the untreated myopia of the goalkeeper, had resulted in the team winning only six games in its last eleven years. But for all their weaknesses, the Furtwangler Kickers held the answer to Max Sponge's problem.

The agreement was that Max Sponge and Oran Phillips should commence business in the 'sporting holiday' sector, inviting football teams from abroad to come to Stockholm for a holiday which would include a soccer match against a local team, a historical tour of the city, and some late-night entertainment of the kind that holidaying soccer teams tend to enjoy. The Furtwangler Kickers would provide the sporting opposition (their age to be kept a secret until the foreign team arrived, although Max considered it good etiquette to make it easy for the visitors to win), Max Sponge's girls would provide the late-night entertainment, and now Rory Brophy would act as a guide to the sights of the city in which he had only spent three days. It was an ideal arrangement for everyone. The Kickers would be paid for their services, the money to go towards the construction of a new dressing-room, as their old one had been demolished with a sledgehammer by an irate landlord for non-payment of rent for four years. Max Sponge would see a dramatic upturn in his business and Rory, well Rory Brophy would be able to earn money as a guide and perhaps get his own apartment.

Rory's only problem was that he knew nothing about Stockholm. Only hours beforehand he had thought it was in Denmark. A visit to the local library was in order, he decided, but Max Sponge dismissed the idea. 'Who will know if what you are saying is correct? This is your chance to rewrite history. I'll give you the names of some famous figures from Swedish history and you can do the rest. These people will be footballers, remember. They're here to play football and fraternise with some Swedish women. The guided tour is merely to give a flavour of the place, to add some respectability to our little venture. And it will give them some names of people and places to take home to their wives and girl-friends.'

So Rory Brophy heard for the first time the names of people such as Agne the Warrior, who was hung by a group of Finnish prisoners led by his wife Skjalf on an island that now forms part of Stockholm; King Gustav Vasa, who made Stockholm the capital of Sweden in 1523, and Gustavus Adolphus, who had made it the capital of an empire by the time of his death on the battlefield of Lutzen in 1632. With these and a handful of other names, Rory Brophy set about recreating Stockholm's past. To get over the problem of too few names for too long a span of history (it was clear from landmarks that Stockholm was an ancient city), he simply added a few more generations to each name. Hence there were five Gustav Vasas and an imperial line of Gustavus Adolphuses that ran as long as he could hold his audiences' attention. Great architectural masterpieces built by people like Nicodemus Tessin were attributed to rulers who never existed. The Drottingholm Palace, for instance, was commissioned by Gustavus Adolphus IX to celebrate his marriage to Queen Ingrid of Iceland in 1790.

The venture began very well for all concerned and

Rory earned enough money to rent his own apartment off the Birger Jarls Gatan, where he could look down and watch the city recreate itself over and over each day. He would watch all the people hurry to work in the mornings and go home tired in the evenings like prides of lions after an unsuccessful hunt. What a city he had crawled up out of the satsumas to enter. It had given him things he had never dreamed of. His new record-player and his autographed picture of the Furtwangler Kickers, for instance, which he hung on the wall near the entrance to his apartment beside the reproduction painting of Skjalf who killed her husband in the name of Finland. In the mornings he would sit with Max Sponge at one of the cafés and discuss what would happen in the history of Stockholm that day. 'Let's make Gustavus Adolphus VIII a notorious womaniser who dies of gonorrhoea,' suggested Max. 'Let him have left the city rife with rumours of illegitimacy. No monarchy worth its salt is without pretenders to the throne.'

Some mornings they were joined by Oran Phillips on his break from work as a clerk at the office of Linneaus & Anderson, Solicitors. Oran would immediately begin to talk about football. 'To hell with this pretender to the throne stuff,' he said once. 'Make Gustavus Adolphus VIII the father of Swedish football. Have him sent to England as a young boy by his father. Make him an unhappy child because Adolphus VII was a tyrannical father who sent his eldest son away to school so he would not interfere with his father's exploitation of the peasants. So the young heir had a rotten time until he saw a few kids kicking a ball in England and he found a meaning to life. Football became his friend. These guys will love this – there's nothing they like more than the image of soccer as the game of the downtrodden, even if he was the heir to the throne. So he brought the game back to Sweden and within a few years all the poor people were playing it. When Adolphus VII dies of gangrene, or something like that, his son becomes the patron of the game in the country. A ruler much loved by his happy, kicking subjects. There you are, give them that, they'll love it.'

So this was how Rory Brophy had spent his life since his disappearance. For the best part of two years he had collected soccer teams from their hotels, after they had beaten the Kickers in the afternoon, and escorted them on a two-hour guided tour, concocting history as he went. Then he had brought them back to their hotels for an evening meal. After they had eaten, he never saw them again. Max Sponge would arrive and welcome them to the Stockholm night. Rory never got to see the more *risqué* side of the business, but anyway the morality of their evenings did not bother him – he had no opinion on it. Everyone was a winner in a conscience-free frame of mind.

It was funny to think of the mystery he had left behind after his disappearance. To think that at about the time the useless Inspector Throckmorton was officially declaring him a missing person, Rory was climbing up out of the satsumas into the daylight and dashing off from the ship's captain. Or when we were attending the special mass in Missus Brophy's front room, he was busy perverting the course of Scandinavian history to a crowd of soccer players. 'What a cad you are, Rory,' I thought to myself. 'I thought you might be alive all right, but not this alive.'

It was after explaining the nature of his existence

over the past two years that Rory Brophy outlined his reason for writing to me. It was because Max Sponge had decided that he should expand his business. They could handle a second team for which he needed a second guide. 'Someone with good English that can talk a lot of rubbish,' was how he specified it to Rory. The first thing that came to Rory's mind was our conversation in my front room when I explained my encounter with the spirits beyond. He told Max Sponge what I had said to him. This was the first time the contents of the conversation had gone beyond the two of us, but he felt I would thank him if it resulted in an excellent job in Stockholm. 'Jesus, that guy sounds like a real donkey,' said Max Sponge. 'Write to him and see if he's interested.' So Rory had written to me to offer me the chance of a new beginning just as he had had. He was returning the favour for the times I had not joined in the mocking he had always suffered. I had never left the imprint of my hand on his back. Here was Rory Brophy, the butt of relentless jokes, offering me a job, a place in his disappearance, the role of supporting actor in his mystery. But no matter what decision I made, I must not tell anyone I had heard from him. The letter must be destroyed. What a crazy situation this was. The very last person we all believed could make an exciting life for himself was inciting me to join in his magnificent crime. This was indeed a genuine show of trust in my integrity. I had in my hand an exhibit capable of destroying his second life, but he had judged my character to a tee. I had agreed after reading the first sentence to keep it a secret no matter what I decided, even if it meant taking the knowledge to my grave. Having recorded his address, I took the letter to the grate in the kitchen, struck a match from the box on the mantlepiece and set fire to the paper. I suppose everything turns to ashes in the end.

4 Tea

Despite the construction of the flyover and the fact that it darkened everything, my mother still went to the box-room in my grandfather's house to sit at the place where she was born. The traffic hurtled past the side and the back of the house now, heading for the airport and the sea. The room had become a noisy place and this angered her. It meant she had to concentrate harder to reach the peace that had been the tonic for her through some difficult years. I rarely went to the room any more, finding it always dark and cold and almost sinister. It was more difficult to understand how she kept going there and coming away feeling better. It was a dead room to me, but I'm sure this just went to prove that the acquisition of a spiritual strength was beyond the physical characteristics of a place. It was a combination of just being there and the memory process she experienced which made it special. I think she believed that she could hold back time in this one place, as if it defied its surroundings where everything was in a state of flux. Buildings were going up and coming down. The cars were going faster. The children's language was getting worse (at least that's what she maintained). And we were all getting older. As we did, the significance of that room seemed to dwindle. It was only in her mind that it maintained a place in the overall plan of things. Progress demanded that she now wear a heavy jumper and work harder in her little time warp to reach that state of mind which released the elixir of inner contentment.

The existence of this room made it easier for me to consider the offer which Rory Brophy had made me. Or perhaps I should say that it made it easier for me to accept the offer than it would have been for others. For it was always in the back of my mind that, should I abscond without a word to anyone, it would be easier on my mother than it had been for Missus Brophy. I knew that she would go to the box-room and understand that the world was a cruel place at times from which no one was perpetually immune. I have to say that this was a major factor in my considering the idea of vanishing. I did not have it in me to inflict the same torment on her as Rory had done to his own mother. It was inconceivable that I could do such a thing. There would have to be something for her to hold on to which would keep her sane through the stupid announcements of Inspector Throckmorton and the wild-goose chase initiated by the nymphomaniac tracker dog Wino. She would have to be able to rise above it all through a greater understanding of love than that provided by the physical presence of someone. The box-room provided me with an accomplice.

Unfortunately for Missus Brophy, she had no such place. Born seventy miles from the city in a house which no longer stood, she could not exclude the calamity which had befallen her by returning to the place of her birth. She had an unfortunate disposition for a woman in her predicament. This was a trust in man's ability to answer difficult questions by the application of brains, time and energy. She believed that all things had a reason and just because we do not understand everything now does not mean that no reason exists. For her, blind faith in God was too easy and not enough. Someday we would know everything about everything. It would take a long time, but the garden of mysteries in which we wandered did have a back wall and one day we would reach it.

However, this very rationalism, which some might find praiseworthy, was the cause of her inability to get over the disappearance of her son. Events without apparent reason really hurt her. She became obsessed with finding the answer and, in the nature of all such rational people, it was an obsession which would last until the mystery was solved. In the cause of this answer she waned with the passing months and years. The thought that something dreadful had happened to Rory ate away at her. Perhaps his body had been abused and then dumped somewhere, his skeleton to be found in the foetal position in years to come by a man walking his dog. She developed a habit of searching secluded places for him.

On the occasion of Rory's next birthday after his disappearance, when they had eaten dinner at the table with the empty space, Missus Brophy left the house announcing that she was going for a walk. When she had been gone for some hours, Mister Brophy became concerned that his family was vanishing one by one from the face of the earth. At half past ten there was a knock at the door and he could see a large figure in dark clothes through the frosted glass.

It was Inspector Throckmorton returning his wife to him. She had been found wandering through the back lanes around the French market searching behind all the big iron rubbish skips calling, 'Rory, Rory, it's me, Mama. I have some rabbit-stew ready for you, come on now, come on home.' Buddhism teaches that the spirit of a person who does not receive a proper burial wanders in loneliness for eternity. It appeared that the opposite was the case for Missus Brophy and that it was she, the living, who was doomed to such a fate.

More embarrassing for Mister Brophy than having his wife escorted home by the police was the time she was brought home by Maude Tennison, 'The Mother of Morons'. It was an early Saturday evening in early winter, just after dark, and she had disappeared from the house without a word to anyone. She had left the dinner boiling on the cooker and it was only the smell that alerted her husband, who ran into the kitchen to find it deserted and thick with steam and the scent of scorched metal. He knew immediately that his wife had taken off again in search of Rory. It was pointless to go looking for her – she could be anywhere. There was no use, either, calling the police. Inspector Throckmorton was growing very impatient with this case because it was an acute source of embarrassment to him. There was nothing to do but sit and wait and pray a little that she would not be attacked or fall down a dark hole.

She had been gone for two hours when a knock came at the door and there was Missus Brophy standing with her head hung down low in defeat and her arms held by Maude Tennison, who had found her sifting through the rubble of the three derelict shops at the corner of Gibson Avenue and the Donohue

Mile. Those places had been checked and checked again during the original search, but this would never satisfy Missus Brophy. The possibility that her son could have been murdered and the body discarded somewhere after the place had been searched meant that there was no location which could be definitely said not to contain Rory's body. This was a search without end and which went round and round and round again.

Whenever the enormity of her loss became too great she would have to go and look for him somewhere. This Saturday evening, as the bottom of her saucepan melted away, she had gone to this place and begun her search in the ruins of what had once been the thriving hairdressing salon of Missus Imelda Green, who was no more. There were those who said that she had been too successful in business and, for a woman of her constitution, overworked herself. But history had been very good to Imelda Green. You might not think it, but history and hair have a lot in common. At the time that Missus Green was establishing her business, the country was going through a state of turmoil. With the departure of the colonialists, the locals had only themselves left to fight, which suited them perfectly, and there was a prolonged period of war which historians had broken down into two civil wars, three military coups, an army *putsch*, two workers' revolts, one peasant revolt and an army wedding which had got completely out of control. As is always the case, there were those who gained from such chaos. Munitions manufacturers and undertakers are obvious examples, but hairdressers are also blessed with immunity from the deprivations of war. As her husband pointed out to me during this period,

'Where there's a new widow, there's a new hair-do.'
In fact, more than one new hair-do. The frequency of
funerals at that time proved a gold-mine to Missus
Green's business as the widows arrived to have their
hair done for the funeral accompanied by entourages
of sisters, sisters-in-law, mothers, female friends,
daughters and other general hangers-on who would
accept any excuse to have a new hair style. Missus
Green was very shrewd about this and offered dis-
counts to funeral groups. In the years of chaos she
made a lot of money.

As the country moved into a period of more stable
government, Missus Green did not find it had a detri-
mental effect on her business. There were the election
campaigns, three of them in the first eighteen months
as the first two proved inconclusive. Then there was
the referendum on the new constitution. This was
followed by two elections for the presidency. The first
President of the Republic was seventy-nine when
elected. He was an old campaigner of the wars of
independence and was considered a father of the
nation. Though doubts were raised about his age at
the time of his election, it was considered that the
purely ceremonial nature of the job would not prove
too much for him. He dismissed the comments by
saying that he had fought all his life to see this day and
he was not about to die before he could enjoy the
fruits of his labour for a few years. Unfortunately for
the first citizen, his heart had other ideas and he died
of massive coronary failure eight weeks into office.
His funeral brought the women back to Missus
Green's salon as they prepared to mourn their leader.
They were all back again some weeks later at the
beginning of the new campaign and again at the

inauguration of the second president. Even without such goings-on, peacetime was good for the hair business, as it was the custom for the women to receive any profound news about the state of the nation with a visit to the hairdressers.

When it appeared that all the wars and elections and profound news announcements were over, at least for a while, Missus Green had to consider how she might maintain business at the level it had reached during the previous years. She decided on two courses of action. First, she would open her business to young boys (up to then no male had ever had his hair done on her premises). The second decision was to invest in a huge brown leather chair that swung up and down, left and right, backwards and forwards, and was so comfortable that people had difficulty staying awake in it.

The chair was a major investment as it was state-of-the-art and had to be specially shipped from the United States. Missus Green's thinking was that it was no more than a business like hers should have. She was, after all, an artist in hair, a sculptor of incredible headsets, the doyenne of coiffeuses, an inventor of wavy menageries. No other person in the country had seen as many crowns as she. She could recognise women by looking at the tops of their heads as easily as by looking at their faces. So she ordered the chair from America and when it arrived it took three strong men to manoeuvre it into the shop and bolt it to the concrete floor. 'Jesus, this thing would make me seasick,' said her husband after his first go in it. 'That's not surprising,' she said, 'you get seasick washing vegetables.' 'It's like something a psychiatrist would have,' he said. 'Is that what you think, that you're some sort of shrink?' 'I suppose I am in a way,' she said. 'We have much in common, hairdressers and psychiatrists. We both deal with problems of the head.'

Missus Green's decision to invest in the big chair proved a stroke of genius. People came from miles around to sit in it and be pampered. Little boys were brought by their mothers and had to sit on a plank of wood placed across the arms of the chair. They had the backs and sides of their hair shaved to the skin, but the hair on top was left a little longer so it could be doused in oil and flipped over.

Missus Green was a fortune-teller of hair, a fore-teller of baldness. She could tell by the hair of a young boy whether he would lose his crop in later years. Three-year-olds perched up like budgies on the plank might be doomed to baldness. Not wishing to upset the youngsters with her prognoses, Missus Green would turn to the child's mother sitting on the bench along the wall and mime the words 'He'll be very bald' with terrible contortions of her face. 'Do you hear that, Danny boy?' said Monica Gibbons, when the future of her son's hair was outlined to her. 'You're going to be bald like your daddy.' The child's response was a smile so wide that the sides of his mouth disappeared off the edges of the mirror in front of him. 'Just like your daddy, Danny boy, more hair up his nose than he has on his head.'

Missus Green's business continued for some years after the arrival of the big chair. It remained successful until the day her legs could take no more. All the years of standing behind heads had taken their toll, and she now had fallen arches and varicose veins that encircled her legs like boa constrictors. This was the end of her career. The woman who had made people beautiful ended her life in the house above the shop that could not fail, with only one leg left and reading a copy of *Hairdressers' Monthly*. At her funeral service there was a marvellous collection of hair-dos and the priest said of her that 'She had lived for hair. It had been very good to her and she had surely died with hair on her mind.' After her death, the shop fell derelict. The brown leather chair was taken out and put in a safe place, although the base had to stay because it couldn't be moved. Rory's mother would now wander through the room where she had been assured that her son would always have a healthy crop of hair, calling his name, calling him to dinner, telling him that she would make a special rabbit-stew if he would come out from where he was hiding.

When she did not find him in the ruins of Missus Green's shop, she went next door. This had once been a shoe-repair establishment of a man called Bill Dunion (brother of Malachy, the last man to see Rory alive), who was nicknamed Vasco da Gama. In the last election, Vasco da Gama announced his intention to run as an independent communist. He said that the country had been destroyed by nationalism and factionalism which had set brother against brother. What was required was a broader view which had a perspective of the world outside as being important too. He was not a very intelligent man, and when he spoke his nerves made him stammer so much that people would giggle and he would have to plead with them to stop. The one figure in history who fascinated him was the astronomer Nicolaus Copernicus, who had been the first man to suggest that the Earth was not the centre of the Universe and that, in conjunction with all the other planets, the Earth revolved around the sun. Copernicus was to prove a useful model for Vasco da Gama. He likened the nationalists to those who had chastised Copernicus for this theory, believing their small place to be the centre of everything. 'We are simply a tiny part of a whole human race,' Vasco would say. 'Our future lies with the outside world, not with the petty squabbling of the disgruntled factions in the army and the political parties who disagree over the most menial of things for the sake of argument.'

Vasco was convinced on the night he announced his intention to stand that his campaign would attract the support of some educated people. On the first day of the campaign he closed his shop at three in the afternoon and sat outside behind a flower-table with pen and paper waiting for people to come and enlist to help him. But in the four hours that he sat there, only three people came to sign up. First there was Sylvie Drummond, who had spent his life drifting in and out of states of sanity, so no one knew if he was completely mad or just so on a part-time basis. Vasco da Gama's Communist Party was the fourth political party Sylvie Drummond had tried to join that day. Being at least half mad he had no political convictions whatsoever. He just loved electioneering because of the posters and stickers which were freely available. The other three parties had turned him down because he had failed to answer the simplest of questions, such as who the party leader was at the time. He had almost been beaten up in the Justice Party local office when he incorrectly guessed that they had lost the civil war. It was only the prompt intervention of an enthusiastic activist in a brown suit and reddish tie that prevented Sylvie's nose being pushed out the back of his head by a man called Sergio Macauber.

Sergio Macauber had been a notorious figure during the wars against the colonialists when he lived in the mountains near the city. He had personally killed forty-two of their troops by squeezing their heads between his knees until their skulls cracked. Forty-two soldiers had met their deaths in a foreign country to the roars of Sergio shouting 'Look, Ma . . . No hands!' He was known as the 'Monster of the Mountains' by the newspapers, whose editors had received threatening letters from him saying that they would suffer the same fate as the soldiers unless they used his nickname, of which he was very proud. But the colonial government put a stop to this publicity and ordered the papers to refer to him by a new name. As well as being notorious for his savagery, Sergio also possessed two very smelly feet. The government decided to demystify this man because he was proving too influential on young males. They sent a circular to the editors informing them he was to be known as 'Smelly Feet Macauber'. This sent Sergio wild with anger and there were those who swore they heard him screaming above the noise of the city-centre traffic as he went on a rampage in the mountains, deforesting half an acre by pulling the young shoots from the ground with his teeth. After the wars, Sergio was given a medal because the Minister for Justice was very frightened of him. Never one to miss an opportunity, the Chief convinced him to become involved in politics, so Sergio was shaved and put into a suit which was too small so his arse stuck out like a chimpanzee's. He was duly playing his part as a kind of fairground attraction at the local Justice Party office on the day that Sylvie Drummond wrongly answered some simple questions. But Vasco da Gama was in no position to be too selective. He could never see Sylvie Drummond winning over people with the force of reason, but he would at least be useful for running around sticking up posters.

The second person to join the new party was Rogy Cullen, who had run a greengrocery in the shop on the other side of Vasco da Gama's from Missus Green's. Two years previously, though, Rogy Cullen had run into financial problems and was forced to close down. It was not that he had run a bad business – indeed, the quality of the produce he sold was second to none. He would awaken the whole street at four in the morning turning the crank-handle of his rusting van and heading off to the markets to buy supplies for the day. What had caused the downfall of his business was the intensity of his friendliness. It was such that no one could bear his company, and when he came to join the Communist Party he spent forty minutes telling Vasco of how much he had always liked him and then another fifteen minutes admiring the craftsmanship of the table Vasco was sitting at. He was particularly impressed by the way the legs were joined to the surface, and told Vasco that he was a man of wonderful taste when it came to selecting furniture, something he had always suspected as he sat in his house and thought to himself how lucky he was to have such a person as Vasco as his neighbour – a man of such integrity and kindness, and learned enough to know of the ancient astronomer Copernicus. He had always thought that such a man as this must also have had the gift of telling a good flower-table from a bad one, and this one he was sitting at was one of the best he had ever seen.

It was during his fifteen-minute discussion concerning the flower-table that a unique event occurred in the history of Vasco da Gama's Communist Party, namely that there was a queue to join. At the moment that Rogy Cullen crawled under the table to have a closer look at the way the legs were joined to the surface, a woman called Roisin Misheveni arrived to sign up. She was a middle-aged woman who came to enlist because she had been left without her husband, who had been killed in the war previous to the one before the last one. Roisin Misheveni had five children to feed and a paltry allowance from the state to provide for everything. She admitted to Vasco da Gama that she knew nothing about communism, so he gave her his illegal copy of *The Communist Manifesto* to read. When she returned it a week later she told him that she loved him very much and asked him to marry her when the election was over.

In amongst the well-financed campaigns of the big national parties, Vasco da Gama stood little chance of winning a seat. He had a lunatic, a bore and a destitute woman as his staff. On the night before the election, Vasco made a final tour of some of the pubs to try to win some votes. It was not to be a happy end to the campaign for the communist. He completed his tour in a place called Arthur Bloss Himself, at closing time. It was here that he was christened Vasco da Gama by an intoxicated refrigerator repair man who was adamant that communism was based on da Gama's writings. In the street outside Vasco was set upon by a gang of drunks who beat him up and called him a 'red prick' before returning inside, leaving the political ambitions of Vasco da Gama lying face down on the frozen concrete. When the votes were counted, Roisin brought Vasco the bad news to his sick bed that he had received only two votes, her own and Rogy Cullen's. When they questioned Sylvie Drummond about where his had gone, he told them that as an officially recognised lunatic he was not entitled to vote. A day later, Vasco da Gama and Roisin Misheveni disappeared with her children and never came back. Missus Brophy now wandered into the shop that had once echoed to the sound of Vasco's hammer on leather and been filled with the smell of new shoes, and she was calling to her son to come home now. It was here that she had been spotted by Maude Tennison, who saw in this event the makings of hours of gossip over the fact that the loss of her son was systematically turning Rory's mother into a person of doubtful sanity.

As well as finding myself in an awkward situation after receiving Rory's letter, I also felt a sense of power at holding something over someone else. It was the power that comes through superior intelligence, and it gave me a tingling feeling to know something that nobody else knew. It was almost enough to make me giggle, but I was quick to realise what this piece of knowledge could do to me if I was not careful. I knew that it could release in me some of the more base forms of human behaviour, such as I believe are common to us all, though some are better at controlling them than others. I could have taken great delight in seeing Rory's mother suffer beneath the weight of her ignorance, and manufactured situations designed to make things worse for her. I knew that the sight of me upset her – not because she did not like me, but because I reminded her of Rory. I could have deliberately engineered 'chance' meetings – following her to the shops and standing outside until she came out for example. Or I could have kept asking her if there was any good news. I was perfectly aware that this power could corrupt if I was not careful, but in a level-headed debate with myself I resolved not to allow that to happen. My piece of knowledge was a double-edged sword. Having rejected the possibility of using it for destructive purposes, I felt I must devise a way of using it in a constructive way which would bring order to the chaos Rory's disappearance had created. It still made me angry that he should have done such a thing, but I believed it might be possible for me to convince him of the harm he had done. I thought that if I could explain to him the consequences of his action, he might reconsider and I could emerge as the glorious mediator whose inspired vision set wrongs to right. If this was to be my course of action, then I had to prepare things. The first step was to respond to Rory asking him to inform Max Sponge that the donkey who had been visited from beyond gratefully accepted his invitation to act as a fraudulent historian.

When considering how I would get to Stockholm, I was not troubled by how I would pay for the fare. My means of getting there were certainly going to be more conventional than Rory's. The idea of jumping from the flyover into a passing truck of satsumas did not appeal to me – in any case, how would I know where it was going? Satsumas were the country's most important export. They were shipped all over the world, so my chances of landing in a truck with fruit bound for Sweden were very slim. I would go by sea all right, but not as a stowaway. I would pay for my ticket – or rather, somebody else would.

The nature of what I increasingly looked upon as a mission rather than a trip left me with more room to manoeuvre than would ordinarily have been the case. I was still young – almost out of my teens – but since the age when it is possible to be so, I had been burdened by the weight of a heavy conscience. Sometimes that can be a terrible thing, and I believe that mine was delivered to me early – as a young boy I definitely suffered from premature conscience. It robbed me of many things that young boys enjoy doing. Literally enjoying the fruits of a burgled orchard never came to me. It was not that I didn't take part, but that I never enjoyed doing it. I seemed to be aware, and alone in this, that what we were doing was committing a crime and that someone would suffer as a result of our actions. This worry was compounded by the fact that all the small orchards nearby were owned by old people. This seems to be a worldwide phenomenon, perhaps a result of evolution: small orchards are always owned by the elderly. Most of them had also lost their spouses, so old widows and widowers would go into their gardens in the morning and discover their crop had been stolen. All I could think of as we devoured our spoils was of an old person in tears in the morning, probably returning inside and picking up a picture of their departed loved one and wondering why the world always picked on them.

I was never sure if the others recognised my unease in those situations, but it strikes me that they must have done. I was always the one who argued for moderation. I was always the one to suggest playing football again. But my peers seemed every day to build up this head of steam which could only be released by doing something on the criminal side of mischievous. When all else failed, I would plead the case of the one who was about to become the victim. This was never easy as most of the old ones who owned the orchards were cantankerous, and you wouldn't have to work hard to convince yourself that they deserved it. The job of trying to protect such a vulnerable booty had turned them into nasty people because they knew from the outset that they would lose and that their only possible victory would be the Pyrrhic one of taking a saw to all of the trees. Despite the horribleness of these orchard owners, I still made attempts to prevent the raids; but I was the lone protester outside the walls of the prison at dawn on execution morning. I was the padre who accompanied the condemned man to the gallows and stood beside him as they took his life away. I was the sea-stack stood where the raging sea bashed against the cliffs. But I never had it in me to go the whole way and suffer the taunt of 'chicken'. After I had done my best, I would do as the proverb suggests, and join in. But I did so with a heavy conscience that roared at me through every second of the heinous deed: 'This is wrong, this is wrong.'

With such a burden to carry, I turned into a boring youth. My mother even commented once on the fact that I had never received a serious injury while taking part in a ludicrous stunt. She said it almost with an air of disappointment. I felt I had let her down and considered going into the back garden and hurling myself from the top of the cherry blossom tree, but with my luck I would probably have hit the ground without sustaining so much as a graze. I would be completely unbruised and walk away from the scene feeling very stupid, the little dent in the grass being the only souvenir of my attempt to achieve the glorious recklessness of boyhood. Now that I was approaching the age when conscience is supposed to play a part in every decision you make, I felt more at ease and less freakish. Indeed, I think the early development of my conscience meant its power to prick had already peaked. I was able to approach the problem of financing my mission with less bother than when robbing apples. The fact that this was a mission of mercy – on which I would try to persuade Rory to come home, or at least, to make contact with his heartbroken family – meant that it would not be so bad if I obtained the money under false pretences and with no intention of paying it back.

As I have said, in my late teens my conscience was on the wane from overuse. I was running out of the stuff and was glad of the fact because it bored even me. I could think of only one place where I could lay my hands on the cash I needed. On the evening of the day I posted my letter to Rory announcing my acceptance of his offer, I sat in our front room with my mother and father and watched *Old Friends and New*. This was the country's favourite soap opera, and between seven and half-past everything stopped for it. A few months earlier, the fragile stability of the Republic had almost been lost when the transmission froze in mid-episode. It could not have got stuck at a worse moment, for it happened during a scene in which Oranche O'Higgins was conducting an argument with her husband Phillip. She was the sweetheart of every man in the nation. The inside of half the locker doors in the Republic were adorned with the picture of her which appeared in *Fresche Murabe*, which translated means 'the information gathered by a spy written down after a debriefing'. Oranche appeared in this photo wearing a white blouse (is there a woman in the world who does not look good in a white blouse?), of which the top two buttons were undone. The delicious little pips on either side gave away the secret that she was wearing no bra. She gave reason to the lust that men feel for women, she was the end of evolution. We had all come all the way from brainless, spineless, legless, armless, ridiculous amoeba and ended up with Oranche O'Higgins. She had ended up with her husband Phillip, who never appreciated her. He was scurrilous and treated her despicably. For months the nation had willed her to take a stand. She was carrying his child and had to sort out once and for all if he was going to behave himself, or if she must leave him and go somewhere where the child would be protected from his drunken bouts. After months of subservience she finally plucked up the courage and took him to task. She really had a go. In every house in the Republic, people were perched on their seats shouting and wringing their hands saying, 'She's doing it, she's doing it.' She was shouting so much that Phillip was speechless. The bastard was meeting his match, and then it happened. When the camera was close up on her face the screen froze. It caught her with her mouth wide open and one of her eyes shut tight. It was a horrible sight. In an instant the beautiful Oranche O'Higgins was transformed into a monster with a face that could round up cattle. There was almost another civil war.

Now all that was history, and we were watching the

episode in which she had her baby. Phillip had gotten the message and he was behaving himself. He even ran for the doctor when the crucial moment arrived. The physician came to his front door buttoning up his trousers, complaining that every time he went to the toilet someone gave birth. His defecating was constantly being interrupted by childbirth and he could only conclude that there was some telepathy between things that travelled downwards through humans on the way to the outside world. Then there was a commercial break and an advertisement for satsumas in which lots of the fruit were dressed in traditional dress from around the world. There was one with a stetson, one in a kilt playing bagpipes, another in a sarong, and they were all singing a ditty. During all of this my mind was on other things. I was contemplating how to get my fare. When I had rehearsed it over and over in my head, I got up and left the room. When I exited the front gate I turned right and headed for the house of Davy Tolan 'with the rotten teeth'.

Davy Tolan was the man who gave the lie to a theory that had developed in my mind over a period of years without my being conscious of its growth. It was a sort of sedimentary theory, comprised of bits of observations I had made which drifted down to the bed of my mind and were compacted beneath the weight of everything else which occupied me, until they emerged as one single theory which held true until the day I met this man. Up until this meeting, I had believed there was no such creature as a man with both lots of money and rotten teeth. But Davy Tolan was a curious hybrid who possessed seemingly endless amounts of money and a mouth of brown teeth. He was a northerner, and the northerners are famed for their business acumen (the Chief was a northerner). Like all good businessmen, his wealth-creating skills he kept to himself. If anyone asked him where he got his money, he would reply with nothing more precise than, 'a bit of this, a bit of that.' Davy Tolan with the rotten teeth was the latest in a very long line of Davy Tolans. He was also likely to be the end of that line, for he was well into his fifties and single. You would imagine that a man of his wealth would have found a wife without much difficulty, but the combination of his miserly reputation and his woeful choppers had left him a bachelor. His one passion in life was history and in our country there was no shortage of it. I once asked him why he liked it so much (the rooms of his house were sinking beneath mounds of history books). 'What do you do if you find yourself in a dark room and you feel threatened?' he answered. 'You look behind you, don't you?' The way the country was at that time, we all kept looking behind us.

My first encounter with Davy Tolan with the rotten teeth had been four years earlier. There was a period in the history of the country known as the 'Religious Wars'. The man who taught me history in school was not particularly interesting to listen to. He had a monotonous voice which put people to sleep and so large chunks of history were missed. I dozed through the whole of feudalism. This led to big problems, especially with essays. Four years previously I had found myself having to write on the nine Religious Wars. My notebook took me up to the Third War without difficulty. During the Fourth War the writing was more slurred and illegible, and by the beginning of the Fifth War, all records had ceased – I was asleep again.

My father suggested that I go and see Davy Tolan with the rotten teeth because he would be able to tell me everything I needed to know. The idea of going and knocking on the door of the man who had always been regarded as strange did not appeal to me, but my father insisted. He had spoken to Davy Tolan with the rotten teeth on many occasions and could not understand my hesitation. He was a perfectly decent man; it was just that people misunderstood him. So I found myself at the door of his house, and when I knocked on it the noise reverberated through the building as if it were completely empty. I thought that Davy Tolan with the rotten teeth must have no belongings or souvenirs. No pictures of loved ones because no one loved him. I was on the point of leaving when the door opened and he looked out at me and smiled so his brown teeth were clearly visible. He was smaller than I had thought – smaller in fact than I was, so if things turned bad I could at least beat him up and run for it. I gulped a last breath of air and told him that I had come about the Religious Wars.

The evening was a revelation to me. I found him funny and knowledgeable. He gave me tea and biscuits and sat me in a deep leather chair in his back room. I felt fine after the tea (my fears about suspicious substances being mixed into it proved unfounded). There were books all the way from the floor to the ceiling, but he did not have to consult one of them before commencing his account of the Religious Wars. He began by reference to the Hanging Oak at Cooltree, which had played a symbolic part in most of the wars as it became the instrument of highest execution. It had fallen as an acorn during the first of the nine wars, and by the time of the Third War it was suitable for hanging heretics. This was the war of the post-schism schism, between the pro-Gregorians and the anti-Gregorians. It was the first war in the country in which gunpowder was used. The cannons and gunpowder sent to the pro-Gregorians won them the war, because this powerful new weapon devastated the fortifications of the anti-Gregorians – which were designed to stop arrows and sling-shots, not balls of metal propelled by the substance they christened 'Satan's mascara'. But the vanquished gained revenge in the Fourth Religious War between the neo-anti-Gregorians and the post-pro-Gregorians. During that war the rain fell with such intensity that the bogs swelled up and doubled in size. It dampened the gunpowder of the post-pro-Gregorians, rendering it useless, and their opponents' dexterity with the old weapons proved sufficient to give them victory. They now used the tree that fell as an acorn in the First War to dangle the new heretics from heights that exceeded those from which the previous heretics had swung, because the tree had grown in the interim. This historical feature was written to music by the songsters who entertained the neo-anti-Gregorians in their tents on the bitter nights, when they drank to the swinging heretics and gave birth to folklore. So it continued until the Ninth Religious War. Each time the latest heretics were brought to the oak at Cooltree for hanging and each time they swung higher than before. Listening to the wars described in this way brought history to life for me. Davy Tolan with the rotten teeth talked about the subject like a father does about his son. When he had finished, he told me about the long line of Davy Tolans.

It was eighty Davy Tolans ago that the first of them

had crossed the sea to the north and begun the reclamation of the land from the bogs. Since then there had been Davy Tolan the Greater, son of the original Davy Tolan. It was Davy Tolan the Greater who established the Tolans as the foremost family in the north. He had biceps the size of a cow's neck and he reclaimed the land from the bogs by blowing so hard that the water rushed back to the sea. He had a son, Davy Tolan the Lesser, who almost destroyed everything they had achieved. He was senile from inbreeding, so after him the practice was abandoned and within a few generations the Tolans were again the most brilliant and beautiful of all the northern families. As evidenced by Davy Tolan the Chieftain, perhaps the most famous of them all. He was a man of stupefying attractiveness to women, who congregated around him and offered him nights of unimaginable passion if he would go to bed with them. His wife made him grow a beard to hide his handsomeness; but to no avail, for the women found his hairy animal features even more attractive. Even the cows in the fields were in love with him, and they herded towards him whenever he appeared. There had been many more Davy Tolans since then: the Patriot, the Hero, the Swimmer, the Shot, the Writer, and so on. 'And what about you?' I asked him. 'What will your nickname be?' The question upset him. 'I would like to be called the Historian or even the Millionaire, but I think that if I do go down as anything it will be Davy Tolan the Last.'

I could never tell him that he had a nickname which was no less offensive, but he was clearly upset at the imminent end of his line. He told me once, in strictest confidence, that it troubled him so much he had contemplated rape. He would hand himself over to the police immediately after the crime and pay for the counselling and maintenance that his victim would need. That was how desperate he had become at one stage, but this horrible idea had mercifully lasted only a short time.

That was the beginning of an unusual relationship – no, I will call it a friendship – which I had with Davy Tolan with the rotten teeth. Sometimes when he saw me pass his house he would call me in and tell me some new fact he had discovered. 'Did you know that Peter Chest [a nineteenth-century political figure] was the great-grandson of the brother-in-law of the King of France?' or 'I'm almost positive that Ernesto IV reigned for one hundred and ten days and not one hundred and twenty.' He explained the significance of this discovery, which I didn't understand, but it was something to do with there being two kings at the one time, and also an unfortunate mistress being put to death for having had sexual intercourse with a monarch who must have been buried at the time.

Davy Tolan with the rotten teeth had misunderstood the reason why I had gone to see him in the first place. He seemed to think it was because I had an abiding passion for history and wanted to be his protégé. This was not the case at all. I have to admit, though, that he made the subject superbly interesting when he spoke of it, and when he called me to his house to reveal another gem of knowledge, I never had the heart to refuse. It was conscience again. But now, walking towards his house with the price of a boat fare to Stockholm on my mind, I thanked that conscience and the patience I had shown him over the years.

During all of those historical tours with Davy Tolan with the rotten teeth's knowledge, during which I sat in the big leather chair sipping stewed tea with too much sugar in it (I think he was unclear about which was the teaspoon and which the dessert), with the smell of the ageing paper of his huge book collection filling the room – from all of this I developed a better understanding of his mind than anyone else. I guessed that he was not a miser, as everyone believed. It wasn't the spending of money which upset him, but the wasting of it on frivolous things which could not be justified. Indeed, despite what everyone said about him – and especially about his refusal to buy new clothes or to have his house painted so it would not spoil the efforts of all his neighbours who spent their summers up ladders in overalls (his house looked like a bad tooth in an otherwise perfect mouth) – I think he had a better appreciation of the relationship between financial and spiritual wealth than all of his back-stabbing neighbours. The source of his financial wealth was his religion, which derived from the northern culture where his origins lay and dictated that he must work hard and not spend the fruits of his piety surrounding himself with things that gave no greater satisfaction than a sensation of comfort under his backside when he sat down. Not for him such transient things, such sensory tickles, when it was possible to have the full massage by concentrating on the enlargement of his intellect. This could be the only justification for parting with money, and it was a sign of the times he lived in that such fulfilment could be obtained for a fraction of the cost of new chairs and clothes, or the weekly rate of Sam Gorman, 'Painter,

Decorator and Republican'; and that such humble thrift was interpreted as miserliness.

This understanding which he had of the real value of things and, more to the point, my understanding of his understanding, was the Trojan horse that would get me into his wallet. He was thrilled that I had developed such an interest in history, Swedish history at that. He admitted to not knowing much about it, but thought it very broad-minded of me not to confine myself to the history of our own country. He was particularly impressed by all the library books I had brought with me (a stroke of genius on my part). When I showed him the (false) letter I had received from my long-standing Swedish pen-friend promising me an historical tour of Stockholm if I could get there for a weekend, the whole idea so excited Davy Tolan with the rotten teeth that I thought for one moment he was going to suggest that we both go. Being kindred spirits, enthusiastic members of the fraternity of historians, it would be an ideal weekend. But the thought did not seem to have occurred to him and when I slipped (like a cloth over a well-polished table) from the part of our discussion explaining my interest in Swedish history, into the part where I asked whether he would finance the trip if I would pay him back, he never blinked an eye. He was, in fact, engrossed in the index of *Charles XII of Sweden* by R. M. Hatton. When I asked him again, he assured me with a cursory 'Of course, of course' and quickly returned to the book. His reply was similar when I emphasised to him that he must on no account tell anyone of this visit. Still I made him swear on the fellowship of the times past that his lips would remain sealed. It was all as simple as if I had asked him for the time of day.

With the boat ticket in my pocket, I walked home from the city centre because I had a lot of things on my mind. It was a gentle climb which took me an hour to complete. In amongst the more weighty problems of persuading Rory to come home and assessing the possibility that I too might become infatuated with the place and want to stay, there were smaller anxieties that pecked away at me. I had never been on a ship before. The few occasions that I had rowed across the pond at the Ritpish Holiday Camp were hardly preparation for such a journey. What if I was chronically seasick? For all I knew, God might have ordained that the sea and I should never get on, that its constant movement should make my belly and head spin and reduce me to a permanent fixture bent over the railings, sending my dinner into the deep blue below. I might even die before I got there, my entire innards having been thrust up my oesophagus until there wasn't an organ intact within. They would cover me in a sheet and slide me down a plank, so my parting contact with the world would be a tiny splash in a huge ocean, barely audible above the noise of the ship's engines. I was sure this was not how I wanted to go, to arrive at the Gates of Heaven dripping wet and covered in seaweed. How would they recognise me as the one who had passed away on a mercy mission with nothing but good intentions on his mind? And what should I take with me? I was too embarrassed to show my ignorance to the girl in the

TEA

ticket office. There were a hundred questions I
wanted to ask. Are the ships warm? Will I get a cabin?
If I do, will it have windows? Will I have to share with
somebody? If so, will they be nice? These were the
silly minutiae of my journey about which I was
unwilling to consult the girl because she looked the
type who would giggle when I turned to leave.

I confess that by the time I had bought the ticket I
was becoming worried about what I was getting into.
The pace of events during the previous few days had
begun to outstrip my ability to control them. They had
become self-perpetuating, and I had become a passenger on board a ship launched by my own decisions. I
was an explorer thrown from the raft while descending the rapids, foundering in the white water of my
own mind. I was glad, for once, that we lived so far
from the city centre. This had not been the case in the
past. The price of the bus fare to the city centre was
always too much for me to afford, so if I wanted to go
there I had to walk. This meant a two-hour journey
getting there and back, and it was a boring walk.
There were few nice buildings or parks to relieve the
monotony, just small shops one after another for mile
after mile. How they all stayed in business was a
mystery or a miracle, but they did. Some of them were
history itself, part of the folklore of retailing. Like
Monty Bryce, purveyor of vegetables, sweets, cakes
and many things in cans. Monty Bryce's objective in
life was to walk as little as was humanly possible for a
man in his profession – he simply wanted to stand and
watch the world go by the door of his shop. This was
the only place where the light got in. The two windows on either side of it were dirty and stacked with
two big walls of cereal boxes. These represented

Monty Bryce's only attempt at window display, undertaken fifteen years ago. The boxes had remained untouched ever since. The effect of the sun shining on them during the brilliant summers (we used to have) had faded the colours, so it was impossible to know what products they had once contained unless you had a good memory.

In his never-ending search for the formula to an almost walkless existence, he would make a circle of his shop every morning with a cardboard box in his arms and take one of every item he had sold the previous day off the shelves and place it in the box. This tour brought him back to his station opposite the door, where he would unload the contents of the box on to the shelf behind where he stood. This procedure meant that when someone came to buy something, Monty Bryce would only have to turn round and take it off the shelf behind him. In the case of items bought more than once during the day, the regulars would come in and ask, 'Have you sold any sugar today, Monty?' If the answer was 'Yes', then they would go to where the sugar was stocked and take a packet themselves. So that was the way Monty Bryce spent most of his time: a human statue with roundy glasses which reflected the sunlight, carefully allocating his footsteps. His only pair of shoes had been bought to celebrate the birth of his first son, who was now serving as a commandant in the army on the northern border, watching out for cattle-rustlers and refrigerator-smugglers. Monty Bryce had surely earned a place in history as having travelled the shortest distance between his birth and his death for a man of average lifespan.

I went by the door of his shop and appeared as

another fleeting pedestrian in his line of vision. I caused a momentary flicker of light in his life and I looked in to see the two bright spots where the lenses of his spectacles sent back the sunlight. Monty was stationary as ever, thinking about horses, for he was partial to a flutter (sending his youngest son to the bookies rather than walk himself). He was very good at it, too, and had a reputation for his ability to pick winners. This meant that his youngest son was regularly bribed with money and confectionery on his way to place his father's bets by less-gifted punters (one of whom offered him a view of his daughter's growing breasts if he would divulge the winner on Guineas day). It was a procedure which was turning Monty Bryce's youngest into a rich fatty with carnal knowledge belying his age. But the young fatty kept the bribes from his father, who didn't bet for the money so much as the reassurance it gave him that he had a special contact with horses. When he stood behind his counter and looked out of the door of his shop, what he saw were horses going by. Monty Bryce looked at me as I passed and I was a horse to him. Both our minds were wandering: he pondering the beauty of horses, I pondering the speed at which I had undertaken my crusade to bring Rory back, and the possibility that I would not return.

I rose from the city and the river that ran through it. It was a long, slow climb. Half-way up, opposite the gates of the Federal College of Delicious Cookery, I passed Mo Crowley. He was also a shopkeeper, who sold meats of renowned quality. In his hands, the death and subsequent butchery of an animal was brought to the status of art. He was a maestro of meat. He sharpened his knives with the same elegance that a painter fills his palette, and when he filleted steak there were definite surrealist undertones. The boneless meat would drape like Dali's clocks over the side of his butcher's bench. He was, I think, inspired in his work by the beauty of his wife. She was a former infant beauty queen who had been crowned 'The most beautiful of all the beauties' at the national Mothers' and Children's Fair thirty years before. Unlike many young beauty queens, Daphne Crowley did not undergo a metamorphosis into ugliness as she entered her teens. She did not suffer the girlish heartache of pimples and weight problems, her beauty remained constant into her twenties. When she was twenty-seven her father took her to the National Carcass Exhibition (he was a lifelong devotee of dead animals). It was here that she fell in love with the hands of Mo Crowley on seeing him transform a cow swinging on a cleaver into a selection of mouthwatering steaks in twenty-two minutes. On their wedding night she whispered in his ear that seeing him carve meat was superior to orgasm, so Mo Crowley installed a butcher's bench in their bedroom, at which he would dismember a carcass every night in front of his wife.

She was indeed a beautiful woman. She was one of two children, and her younger brother had also been a beautiful baby, but his teens had not been as kind to him as to his sister. He was afflicted by acne of a most severe nature and there were times when his face looked like it was about to burst. But, showing considerable entrepreneurial skills, the erstwhile beauty recognised the fascination which his face had for other children and he charged them money to run their fingers over its surface, which they were always daring each other to do. So as his sister grew into full womanhood and the peak of her beauty, he simply grew a little richer. His sister's looks brought about a big increase in the popularity of the humble rasher amongst the young boys who lived near her – particularly on Wednesday afternoons, when Mo Crowley went to play golf with the Fraternity of Meat Mongers and Victuallers. He was a hopeless but avid golfer, who regularly sent wayward shots into the trees to yells of 'Ah, Mary!' No one knew for sure who this Mary was, so his playing partners concluded that the woman he held personally responsible for the awfulness of his strokes was none other than the second person of the Holy Family, the Mother of God Herself.

Mo's disappearance from the butcher's shop on Wednesdays was quickly noticed, as was the presence of his wife at the till. This explained the rise of the rasher: these 'customers' were penniless and a single rasher was all they could afford. They would always make sure to touch the skin of her hand as they gave her the coins, which they had kissed outside. Little souvenirs from them to her, legal-tender love-charms. She was so beautiful that, since this was before I had ever had the pleasure of making love to a woman, I wondered how it was that Mo Crowley could remain a normal person, having done what hundreds of men wanted to do. Yet when I passed him standing at the door of his shop, he was talking to an old woman about the salt content of southern beef. This is incredible, I thought to myself.

How can this man who has slept with Daphne Crowley have an interest in the salt content of beef? But there he was, engrossed in the subject. I passed him by and continued the steady climb, wondering if sleeping with a woman was all it was made out to be.

My only other recollection of that journey home was meeting the two spinster Tomalty sisters who I passed at the corner of Cemetery Road. The sisters were amateur meteorologists and could predict the weather by sticking their noses into the air and inhaling large sniffs. During my days in infant school (in 'Low Babies' as opposed to 'High Babies'), our teacher would come into the class-room and tell us what the Tomaltys had predicted for that day. As he passed their house in the morning he would bend his head around their open front door and shout 'Well, ladies, what is it to be today?' The answer would come back, 'Not bad today, no need for a fire' or 'The winter's here, light that fire.' This was the basis on which the fire was or wasn't lit when we got to school, and the teacher had more faith in the spinsters' noses than he had in the official forecasts of the meteorological office, who he described as spending their days 'arsin' about with fandangled gadgets'.

He was the kind of man who had his own way of doing things. His view of the world was formed by loneliness from his failure to find himself a wife. When drunk he would confide in someone nearby that he had never known the pleasure of a truly affectionate embrace since his days as an infant. This became an obsession with him and one Monday morning he arrived at the Low Babies class (I had graduated to High Babies at this stage) and announced that from that day on he was introducing a new item to the daily agenda. From then on he would begin the morning by picking up a Low Baby and hugging it for thirty seconds (or from the time the fast hand on the clock went from twelve down to six). The implications of this were lost on the Low Babies, but not on the parish priest, who heard of it from some concerned mothers. The teacher was told that this practice would have to stop; if it did, no further action would be taken. Believing that his intentions had been misunderstood and his fine record of over thirty years service overlooked, the teacher resigned in disgust. In his retirement he contented himself with walking along the streets at tea-time when he could catch glimpses of the conversations and laughter that came from the tables of families eating together. He would return home and open the windows of his sitting room where he would rest and play records as loudly as he could so that everyone would hear and say to themselves, 'There is a man with a great love for music and someone like him must be very happy.' The truth, as you know, was different, as Arnold Armitage (coach of an under-twelve soccer team, amateur actor and next-door neighbour of the teacher) discovered when he heard a series of taps (he counted seventy-eight in every minute) coming from the sitting room of his neighbour. After an hour of this (or 4,680 taps) he decided to investigate by sticking his head in the open window of the teacher's house. He saw his neighbour motionless in the chair with a handkerchief in his hand. A dried-up channel of tears ran from his eyes down to his chin. The hugging teacher had died crying, listening to the voice of Benianino Gigli singing 'Andrea Chenier' by Giordano.

So, the Tomalty sisters passed me at the corner of Cemetery Road. They were in their usual pose, arms linked and heads bobbing up and down like two prairie dogs, noses up and heads swivelling to take the air and keep their weather forecasts up to date. I knew where they were going. They were paying one of their thrice-weekly visits to the grave of Oliver Moorken, Servant of God, the boy who extinguished the light under the Sacred Heart on the wall of his bedroom at the moment of his death. That was in 1934, when tuberculosis was rampant and wizened away the lives of countless thousands every year. Oliver Moorken had contracted the disease and wasted away until he looked like a string-puppet. What stood him apart from others was the manner in which he accepted what was happening to him. He spoke always of God willing it to be so and said that it was not for him to complain or wish things to be any different. He had no fear of death and, when the moment came for him, he passed from life with the smile of a person seeing something that was beautiful for the first time. Beside his deathbed were his mother, a priest and four wailing women. At the exact moment of his death one of the wailers noticed that the light beneath the Sacred Heart on the wall had gone out. This was supposedly an eternal flame – electric but eternal. The significance of this event was not lost on people and within hours of his death, hundreds were kneeling in prayer on the streets outside the house of Oliver Moorken.

Anxious to quieten rumours of divine intervention, the priest telephoned the electricity company to enquire if there had been any interruption in supply at the time of the boy's death. 'Even the faintest flutter, the merest twitch?' he begged, but the engineer he spoke to insisted that there was no reason why the light should have gone out and that no other complaints had been received. He apologised to the priest if any inconvenience had been caused, but that was not what the man of the cloth was looking for. He then knocked on doors and asked people if they had had a similar experience: any interruption in supply, lights going out temporarily, pots going off the boil? But this too was a fruitless line of enquiry. It seemed that the lamp in the bedroom of Oliver Moorken had been alone of all electrical appliances to fail for a short time before somehow being restored to perfect working order.

After his burial, the grave of Oliver Moorken became a place of pilgrimage for thousands of people, especially mothers. It was probably because he was only a child when he died that mothers chose him of all the possible people they could pray to for their special devotions. They came with their children and knelt them at the foot of the grave, touched the fingertips of the children against the soil, and then made them cross themselves. Pregnant women came to pray that everything would be well for them in labour. There was a woman called Monckton who brought her pregnant twenty-three-year-old daughter to the grave. Her daughter had been born blind, and had married a husband who was also blind. Missus Monckton brought her daughter to the grave of Oliver Moorken once every month during her pregnancy, and they lobbied Heaven that the new child should not complete a trinity of darkness, but should be able, in time, to explain in minute detail to its mother and father the kinds of things that went in the wicker baskets they made for a living. At the moment of birth the expectant grandmother rubbed soil from Oliver Moorken's grave on to the belly of her daughter, who screamed so much with pain that her husband had to sit in the garden with his hands over his ears humming a ballad.

When the child was born there were a few seconds of silence during which the whole world seemed to stop. Even the father, who had developed exceptionally keen hearing, later testified that he could hear nothing. The birds stopped in the way they do before an earthquake. A boy who had spent the afternoon rolling a noisy wheel along the street outside stopped. The girls who skipped to the rhythm of songs stopped singing. The father stood up and strained his ears for sounds from the bedroom. He begged them to say something, and just at the moment when the silence had gone on so long he thought everything had been taken away from him, his mother-in-law answered him. She roared at the top of her voice, 'Pupils, pupils . . . she's got pupils.' The father ran to the house, falling over a geranium pot and a bicycle, while his mother-in-law continued to shout out that the child had been born with tiny holes in her eyes where the light could get in, two tiny circles of nothing which she could look out through. It was an early demonstration of the powers of Oliver Moorken. He had not failed the faithful.

Other stories followed about Oliver Moorken – for instance, the miraculous recovery from gastro-enteritis of the eighteen-month-old daughter of the local doctor's wife's sister's husband's brother's nephew, after a pebble from the grave of Oliver Moorken was placed beneath its pillow. The child had almost shit itself into oblivion, but the recovery took place within hours of contact with the powers of the pebble. Another story was told by Esmerelda Finucane (student nurse and collector of alabaster statuettes of saints and ballerinas) of the day Matron Carmencita Carmichael brought a drawing of the face of Oliver Moorken into the ward for terminally ill children at the National Infirmary of the Four Apostles. It was an artist's impression by the painter Daithi O'Conchubhar, who earned a living painting the faces of the children of tourists in the piazza outside the Federal Wax Museum of Remarkable Likeness. Daithi O'Conchubhar had been commissioned to paint the impression by Luke 'The Greyhound' Madden (so-called because he was so quick off the mark), who had spotted the sales potential of an artist's impression of the face of an up-and-coming saint. He paid the disconsolate mother of the boy five times the cost of his funeral in return for the right to reproduce his face on canvas. Luke Madden was not only a very fast greyhound, he was a very rich one too.

In a country so devoted to its dead and so sensitive to the slightest suggestion of sainthood, Oliver Moorken was never going to get much rest. His name was beseeched every day in the prayers of a thousand mothers holding Daithi O'Conchubhar's three-by-four-inch impression, which slipped neatly into their prayer books. Matron Carmencita Carmichael brought in a larger version of it to hang on the wall of the ward, but before doing so she took it to every bed to explain who the boy was. In the bed on the far left-hand side of the room, beside the wash-basin and the linen cupboard, lay a two-year-old boy who in all his life, as far as was known, had never made a sound. Not since the minute Father Milo Savage found him in an empty Rodeo Crisp box, wrapped in a towel on the fifth row back from the altar in his church, a spot to which he had been directed by an anonymous phone call on Shrove Tuesday night, not since that minute had anyone heard the child make a sound. It was as if he sensed that noise led to abandonment, and had vowed not to make the same mistake again. Silence was the price he was prepared to pay, but this was the trapper's noose around the ankle of the fox, and the more he observed his desire to live, the more he wasted away beneath the inertia to which his life condemned him.

To the bed of this boy who was terminally ill from silence, Matron Carmencita Carmichael brought the ten-by-twelve-inch impression of the face of Oliver Moorken, and instantly the Rodeo Crisp boy seemed to recognise who he was, as if inspired by the fraternity of the sick. He lifted up his left hand, sucked in air through his upper teeth and uttered the sound 'va'. Oliver Moorken – the giver of pupils, the healer of the shitting, the creator of words, these were some of the stories which led to his elevation to the position of *de facto* saint, though without official approval. The two sisters I passed at the corner of Cemetery Road had known the boy personally and had been instrumental in the establishment of The League of the Mothers of Oliver Moorken, which campaigned for his beatification. They were also the gardeners of his grave, which they tended meticulously and regularly so that he would have a fitting place to lie.

When I reached home, the house was empty. I was tired from the walking and the heat. My mother had gone to give grandfather his hot milk. He had taken a liking to it in the past year and at half past six he would expect her to arrive with it. I associate this passion for hot milk with the onset of his dementia. It was the first sign that things were beginning to go wrong with his brain. In the early phase of his affliction it was a 'reflexive' illness. (I hope I have chosen the right word here. I remember it from my French studies. There were things called 'reflexive' verbs such as the word *'s'asseoir'*, to sit down. To describe it lexicographically, it had as its antecedent a pronoun which referred to the agent as its direct object.) If this makes no sense whatsoever then don't be upset; my decision to describe my grandfather's emerging insanity as 'reflexive' is probably more confusing than explaining his affliction in simple English. What I am trying to say is that I think he was aware that he was going insane because he could recognise the symptoms. The problem was that the cures he prescribed himself were ludicrous, and could only have been the product of a senile mind. Perhaps now you can see what I mean. He was caught in a circle of which the mug of hot milk at half past six in the evening was the perfect example.

By this stage he was having difficulty remembering my name. I was on a shortlist of five or six which he would rattle off and I would nod my head when he reached the correct one. He told me one day that he was going mad and no doubt about it. I asked him how he knew and he told me about the time he had got into the bath with his smelly socks still on his feet. He said it was like coming out of a dream. He had been sitting there singing 'Who Will Obey Linus Peel?' (an old song from the war previous to the one before the one before the last one) as happy as the day was long, when his merriment was disturbed by the realisation that he still had his socks on. Nothing like this had ever happened to him before and it frightened him desperately, even though he knew it was a common enough ailment with the elderly. But my admiration for him for telling me about this incident turned to worry when he explained the reason for what was happening to him and how he planned to treat it.

He believed his problem arose from the fact that his brain was rubbing against the inside of his skull. This had come about because of the loss of his hair. He described how a human hair was like a scallion. The small bulb at one end was rolled securely inside the skull and acted as a cushion between it and the brain. With the loss of hair, this cushion was no more. The friction caused by the rubbing of bone against brain was leading to incidents such as the 'socks in the bath' one, and this was why he needed hot milk every day. He had noticed, while sitting in the local working men's club talking to Feshty Breathnach about the fast approaching Great Garlic Harvest (when both men would go into their gardens and pull up the huge number of cloves grown during the summer), how a layer formed on the surface of Feshty's cooling milk. At the time he passed no comment, but an idea was taking shape in his brain as he explained to Feshty his recipe for making garlic pepper. He was having a vision of a thick layer of cooling milk forming inside his skull, a perfect panacea for the strain of madness which was entangling him. Within hours of this chance observation of Feshty's mug of hot milk, my grandfather had instructed his daughter to bring him an amount of milk at half six in the evening. When I questioned him as to how he would transfer the milk from his belly to his head, he winked at me and smiled, saying that he had no intention of drinking it. His remedy required it to be massaged into the scalp.

The day of my disappearance was a Monday. It was always a dull day so my vanishing would at least make it interesting. I had to disappear on a Monday because the ferry left very early on Tuesday morning and I had no intention of spending time with the vagabonds and deck-chair hawkers who frequented the street near the port at night. I would get to the departure terminal on Monday evening and sleep in there. I was later to learn of the events which took place when it was discovered that I had disappeared, and they went something as follows. I left at a quarter to seven in the evening when my mother had gone to take grandfather his milk and my father was at his opera rehearsals for *Aida*. I took only a shoulder bag, which I filled with a pair of shoes, trousers, a jumper and a Swedish/English dictionary I had bought in town. I passed virtually no one as I walked down the road behaving like an ostrich, looking at the ground so I could not be seen.

Taking a bus to the port was out of the question. Since the disappearance of Rory Brophy, the bus conductors had taken a keen interest in the question of vanished youths. Having failed to return Rory to his father, their vigilance in the months following his exit was extraordinary, and many young men half-fitting his description had been detained by conductors, who quizzed them scrupulously about who they were and where they were going. It was very commendable that they should show such concern for a colleague, but it became a nuisance for the bus company's public-relations officer, who was inundated with complaints from thin young men about the harassment they had endured at the hands of bus crews. They were soon having to travel with an adult or carry identification documents to prove that they were not Rory Brophy. The crews were a close fraternity and a loss to one was a loss to all. Despite appeals from the company, on-the-spot interrogations continued until a court case in which the plaintiff, Eric Osborne, sued for physical assault, emotional trauma, slander and unlawful detention. Forced to save face, the bus company apologised and suspended the conductor in question, who had noticed the hapless Eric Osborne standing in the stepwell of his crowded number 22A bus. Believing this to be a clever ploy to disguise his true height, the conductor (Samuel Philpott) descended on the terrified passenger and interrogated him with an estimated thirty questions in two minutes. Not satisfied with the answers he was getting, Conductor Philpott branded the now distraught passenger a liar and the whole bus heard it. When Eric Osborne attempted to make a run for it, the conductor overpowered him and tied him to the baggage compartment with the strap of his ticket-dispenser. This would have been excellent work if Eric Osborne had been Rory Brophy, but Eric Osborne was Eric Osborne, and so the conductor was an idiot – and a suspended idiot at that.

This incident brought the issue to a head. It could no longer be tolerated by the bus company as it was losing precious revenue in compensation settlements. In an effort to salvage something from the sorry mess, the company launched a campaign to improve its customer relations by devoting a space in every bus to display the pictures of disappeared people. In this way thousands of passengers every day would become familiar with the faces of missing persons, greatly improving the chances of their being found. However, bus crews had become very involved in the question of missing persons, and as the statistics showed that young males were the most likely to disappear, any of them travelling alone on buses were always treated with suspicion. It was a ridiculous situation, but that was the way things were and why it was impossible for me to travel to the port by bus.

It was a long walk which left me tired and hungry, so I ate some fruit because I felt it was more nourishing than the food from the chippies that abounded around the port and filled the air with the smell of hot grease. I received my first set-back when I was told by a guard that I could not stay overnight at the terminal and so I was left with the task of finding somewhere to spend the night in the rough streets around the port. This was how I met the African-on-the-Run. I passed him while I was searching for somewhere I would be out of sight and trouble. It appeared from the way the shops and warehouses were protected that the tramps were a problem for the owners, who had put up gates across the doorways to keep undesirables from settling there for the night. When I did find a place, it was surprisingly comfortable to begin with. It was a narrow ledge in front of the huge raised doorways of a warehouse where trucks reversed to unload and I lay there like a window-box, having emptied my bag and put on my extra clothes to keep warm. I fell asleep still sniffing hot grease, but when I awoke it was because a smell had invaded my nose that made my stomach feel ill. I opened my eyes and saw a dirty face looking straight at me, which gave me such a shock that I jerked my head backwards and banged it on the steel door behind me. This terrifying face belonged in the make-up room of a theatre or on posters advertising the horror double-bills which I loved to go and see in the Kaleidoscope Cinema on Sunday afternoons. This was the face of the African-on-the-Run, who was not African at all but who did spend a lot of time running.

The African-on-the-Run (and I can only refer to him as that because I never found out his name) had come back to his ledge to sleep for the night only to find me perched up on it. The smell that awoke me was his breath, which was absolutely stinking rancid, so my first reaction was to get myself away from his mouth and upwind if possible. But my first route was blocked by ugliness and halitosis. Was I to die with fright from his terrible face, or be poisoned by his exhalations, before my journey even began? Would I be found dead with a tortured face so that the world would know that I had expired in most uncomfortable circumstances? But this was not to be the case for, despite his appearance, the African-on-the-Run did not have intentions to match. When I jumped off the ledge he ran back from me until he was twenty yards away and then turned around to face me again. I sat back up on the ledge and breathed a sigh of relief that my life was not to be taken from me in that place.

He left me alone when I lay down again. The ledge became less comfortable as I tried to sleep for the second time. When I looked at my watch it was half past one so I had another five hours before the terminal opened. I did eventually doze for I don't know how long before my nostrils again became aware of his disgusting breath. He was right where he had been the first time, staring straight into my face and bending down so our heads were at the same level. I was furious with him for disrupting my sleep again. This was the eve of a most important mission – later even than the eve. I had a long and difficult journey ahead of me and it was crucial that I get some sleep.

I jumped up and yelled at him to go away. I shooed him like he was cattle, but he took an orange from his pocket and gave it to me. The African-on-the-Run's pockets were full of an assortment of fruit and vegetables – he was a walking greengrocer. He gestured me to sit back up on the ledge where he joined me and told me his nickname. He had been called African by the tramps because his skin was dark, though certainly not black. He was a Gypsy, from eastern Europe originally, whose father had come here with one of the travelling circuses which had once been a common sight. When they could no longer pay their way the circuses closed down. The African took to the life of a petty criminal and tramp, and spent much of his time running from the deck-chair hawkers, who were always anxious to beat him up.

I didn't sleep again, but by the time the sun came up the African-on-the-Run was snoring on the ground beneath me. I took off my second layer of clothes and put them back in the bag and walked to the port terminal. It was cold in the morning, but by the time we sailed I was warmer and feeling happy that I could no longer go back even if I wanted to. The decision was made and acted upon, and I was surprised that it had been so easy in the end, with nothing to stand in my way except myself. I had decided beforehand that as I sailed away I would not think of home and what would be happening in the wake of my disappearance. There were quite a few people sitting around on the deck of the ship and I managed to listen to what some were saying, which took my attention away from any inclination to look back.

The Monday morning of the day I left had been designated as the morning of the aforementioned Great Garlic Harvest by my grandfather and Feshty Breathnach. Feshty was one of the great cultivators of all time. The vegetable was his great passion and he consumed it in great amounts, which accounted for two certainties in his life. First, that for a man of eighty-two he was in very good health. Second, that his boast that he had never been kissed by a woman since he discovered garlic at the age of twenty-three-and-a-half was never doubted. He had developed a perfect formula for growing the stuff and the bulbs he grew were the size of sugar bowls. That morning both men went into their gardens and picked the crop. When they compared their biggest cloves it was the same old story for my grandfather, whose champion specimen was dwarfed by the monster that Feshty was able to display – to the traditional taunt that there had been an eclipse when he pulled it from the soil. When they adjourned to the working men's club for lunch, Feshty was not slow to point out to the others that he had again proved himself King of Garlic, and my grandfather had to sit and listen, occasionally pretending to be a good loser by congratulating Feshty on his horticultural achievements.

The day of the Great Garlic Harvest was always the

same for my grandfather. Get up, eat breakfast, pick crop, compare champions, admit defeat, suffer indignation, congratulate Feshty, go home, drink tea. For it was only in the company of tea that his hurt began to heal. It was an important potion in all our lives. Tea was called for in time of celebration and it was a panacea when things were bad. It was part of our blood: our bones wouldn't grow without it. Great Uncle Bernard went to his death demanding it. He had been captain of the rebel forces that shelled the hills near Caligan, where the armies of the First Republic had bedded down for the night of 12 September 1894. They had had their exact position pinpointed to Great Uncle Bernard by Alessandro Tobin, 'The Tout of All Touts', who had fled from the First Republic's camp under cover of darkness so they wouldn't see him, and under cover of their snoring so they wouldn't hear him. Great Uncle Bernard had his canons trained on the spot and opened fire. But it was only one battle in one war and Great Uncle Bernard had picked the wrong side to fight on. In the months after the victory of the First Republic (which led to the establishment of the Second Republic), Great Uncle Bernard was sentenced to death, and in the yard of the military prison at Wickles he had his hands tied behind his back and was asked if he had a final wish. He replied that he did: that they should send the priest away and bring him a large mug of tea instead. His wish was granted but they would not untie his hands, so the firing-squad corporal had to assist him. When he was shot it was said that tea flowed from his wounds as much as did blood.

Grandfather consumed large amounts of tea on the day of the Great Garlic Harvest. The acceptance of another defeat was a serious business requiring plenty of time and tea. The first person to disturb him was my mother when she brought him his mug of hot milk. She had so far been oblivious to the use he was putting it to, but on this day she spied him through the gap between the bathroom door and frame dipping his fingers into the mug and rubbing them over his bald head. He had always taken the mug upstairs when she arrived, claiming that he wanted to sit on the toilet and take it. She had never questioned him about this because she was as aware as anyone that he was going potty and believed it best to allow him his idiosyncrasies. But this day she had taken it upon herself to make his bed and climbing the stairs she saw the movement behind the bathroom door. There he was, cursing Feshty, massaging his crown, and vowing that he would never again be humiliated in the working men's club over the subject of garlic. My mother interrupted him and asked what he was doing, to which he replied, without any semblance of embarrassment, that it was obvious what he was doing – insulating his brain.

This was an upsetting sight for her because she had never seen him do anything as stupid as that before. It was a frightening example of how his senility was creeping in like winter evenings – longer and longer, quicker and quicker. When she returned home there was only one thing for it: obey her natural instinct and reach for the kettle to make herself some tea. She was alone because my father was at his opera practice and I was gone (my vanishment was only an hour or so old). It had not been a good day for her. The Great Garlic Harvest always left my grandfather in a bad temper. She was forever imploring him not to take

part any more. He ought to know that Feshty Breathnach had an empathy with the vegetable which
allowed him to cajole garlic bulbs into growing to
remarkable sizes. On top of the Harvest and the shock
of finding her father rubbing milk into his head
behind the bathroom door, the day had brought other
problems. (In hindsight I chose a very bad day to
vanish. I had not taken into account the temper my
grandfather would be in and the trouble that would
cause. On this point I admit responsibility and shame.
As far as the other events are concerned, I can only
offer as my defence that I knew nothing about them as
they were impossible to predict.)

While grandfather was picking his crop that morning, the postman delivered a letter. My mother was
deeply suspicious of the sound of the letter-box opening as it either meant bills or bad news. She acted as if
she was actually afraid of it in the mornings – that was
when it threw up all over the hall floor – and she
would give it a wide berth as she came down for
breakfast. 'People never write when they have good
news,' she would say. 'I know a bill when I see one,
but when I receive a letter I know something bad has
happened. Somebody's dead or very ill, or it's a relative I don't like [she always claimed not to hate
anyone] who is coming to town and will call.' That
morning the letter-box regurgitated a note from Auntie Beatrice who lived in a town called Amy.

Auntie Beatrice had had the misfortune to go
'around the back' with my mother's older brother
Kevin and had become pregnant in a town in which
there was a received wisdom that genetics were controlled by licence, and that it was physically impos-
ible for a girl to become pregnant until she possessed a

marriage certificate. Uncle Kevin attributed it to the low iron-level in his blood, everyone else said it was pure laziness, but he spent all the daylight hours of his married life sitting asleep in the deck-chair beneath the single apple tree in their back garden. The tree was long dead and popular legend had it that it had died of boredom. He slept from the moment he sat in his chair to mealtimes and then went back to sleep again. A slumbering mass, a colossus in the land of nod, he snored like an earthquake. Cats would never come into the garden because they thought he was a large bulldog. Even the poultry were afraid of him. When he came out of one sleep and prepared to go into the next, he would give off a loud grunt which sent the chickens skeltering for cover. One dropped dead at his feet after wandering too close at the wrong time and getting caught at one of those moments between sleeps. The roar killed the bird instantly. Many of the other chickens displayed behavioural characteristics not associated with their species. There was one Auntie Beatrice christened 'Horsepower' because it chased cars; another she called 'Grim Reaper' because it befriended a fox.

The night that she had gone 'around the back' of the Disco Disco Ballroom with Lazy Uncle Kevin was the turning-point in the life of Auntie Beatrice. Not only did she condemn herself to life with a husband who slept through all the waking hours God sent, but it was also the night of the conception of their eldest son, the troublesome (and I will attempt to be diplomatic as he is my first cousin) Evan Mackey. Evan was by now at a stage in his evolution at which his physique allowed him to bash anyone in his school, and the sordid criminal activity of the Troublesome One had recently come to light in Amy. It was revealed that for two years previous, Evan the Troublesome had been practising the wicked craft of extortion. Under threat of severe beatings many of the collections, produce and artefacts of the citizens of Amy had been making their way from the homes of their rightful owners to that of Evan the Troublesome (notice I continue to use restraint in naming him) through the pupils in his school. One collection was of beer-mats from around the world, formerly the property of Norman Grealey who had spent years in the merchant navy. Norman was alerted to his loss when he went to fetch the pride of his collection, a mat in the shape of an elephant which carried the name of a gentleman's club in Bombay during the Raj. He had gone to get it so he could show it to a travelling ashtray salesman whom he had met in his local pub. Norman went wild with rage when he discovered that his prize beer-mat was gone, along with a dozen or so others. He called all his children into his kitchen and made them swear in front of the picture of the Sacred Heart (lamp working perfectly) that they knew nothing about what had happened to his collection. They all did so, even young Francis, who believed he was sentencing himself to internal fire as a result of his false confession, but preferred that to the consequences of grassing on Evan the Troublesome.

There were other victims too. Businessmen had trouble when it came to stock-taking. Figures didn't add up, items were missing. It continued for two years until Auntie Beatrice found a cardboard box in Evan the Troublesome's wardrobe. She woke Lazy Uncle Kevin to tell him that their son was a thief and an extortionist. His only reaction was to yell at her for waking him with such a trivial matter. 'I thought something was wrong there for a minute,' he said. Auntie Beatrice personally oversaw the return of every single item in the box, along with an apology from Evan the Troublesome, to the rightful owner. Lazy Uncle Kevin was too tired to take part. His abstention from this exercise was very poorly received by the men of Amy. He was awakened one evening by Auntie Beatrice, who had come home to find him fast asleep but covered in blood. He could be the only person ever to have been beaten up and slept through it. It later transpired that his assailants had tried to wake him first but failed, so they decided to beat him up anyway. The news from Amy was another blow to my mother that day. I have to stress again that I could not have foreseen that this letter would arrive when it did. I had always known that Evan the Troublesome was troublesome, but the news that he was involved in extortion (surely one of the most cowardly crimes) shocked even me. My mother sat in the kitchen and read the letter again and (I hope) thought to herself that she was lucky to have me as a son and not my first cousin. This would have been about the time I was walking to the port. There was only one thing for it, of course – she made herself some more tea.

While she sipped the produce of the hills of Kenya there was another storm brewing (if you will excuse the pun). It was taking place in the upstairs room of the Semi-Crotchet pub, which was set aside every Monday evening for use by the Woolf Box Company Operatic Society. The Woolf Box Company was a large employer and my father worked for them as a 'cutter'. The Operatic Society was primarily made up of employees of the company, the male members being split into two groups. This division had nothing to do with voice pitch, as you might have expected. The two groups were loosely known as 'the cutters' and 'the office', the names referring to the parts of the factory where they worked. Over the years, intense rivalry had built up between these two groups of males. Pressure was brought to bear on any new male employee who came to work in either of these areas to join the operatic society. There was the case of Herbert Soso, who came to work for the Woolf Box Company after a lengthy spell of unemployment. This period had left him with little self-esteem and when he got his new job he commenced employment in a frame of mind that prompted him to do everything he was told. During the tea-break at eleven o'clock on the first morning of his employment, Herbert Soso sat in the most inconspicuous spot he could find in the canteen, whence he peered like a First World War infantryman over the top of a tomato and cheese sandwich. 'Herbert,' my father said to him, 'do you sing at all?' Herbert was thinking that he must be imagining things. He paused for some moments before he confirmed to himself that he was in fact being asked a question. After a break of ten to fifteen seconds, during which all activity stopped in the canteen and everyone stared at the tuft of hair rising above the sandwich, Herbert forced out the syllable 'No.' 'Of course you do, Herbert,' my father answered him quickly, and at this stage still good-naturedly. 'Everybody sings. Give us a blast there, Herbert. Sing anything you like.' Herbert almost passed into the next life behind his big sandwich. Too terrified to make any response (and wishing he was back unemployed), Herbert was locked in a kind of pre-death rigor mortis.

My father and his fellow workers waved their hands in front of his eyes and shook him, gently at first but soon violently. Then the company doctor was sent for. He diagnosed that Herbert Soso was in a severe state of shock and gave him a note excusing him from work for three days.

When Herbert Soso returned he was greeted by a barrage of apologies but, mindful of their numerical inferiority in the Operatic Society, the cutters were still anxious to have him enrol. When they did eventually get him to sing (his vocal cords lubricated by six pints of beer and a vodka) it was the most awful sound but there was no alternative but to bring Herbert to the rehearsals. His vote was more important than his voice. In his first three appearances – in *The Barber of Seville*, *Tosca* and *Trial by Jury* – Herbert Soso was instructed to remain surrounded by cutters at all times and just to mime the words. Three operas he had appeared in and never sang a note in any of them.

The tension was immense in the upstairs room of the Semi-Crotchet that Monday evening. All day long, both camps had been preparing themselves for a contest about who would play Turriddu in *Cavalleria Rusticana* by Mascagni. The casting of the main roles was decided after an audition, a debate, and then a vote. The cutters' nominee was Lucha Bellingham. They argued that he had the experience of playing fairly important roles in six productions and that it was time he was given his big break. He had the voice too, a beautiful, mellow tenor's voice. The office nominee was Hector Millmount, the deputy chief of accounts, and a man who knew his opera very well. They argued that Lucha Bellingham was too small, for Clarissa Nocton, who was playing Santuzza (Turriddu's girl-friend), was three or four inches taller than Lucha and it would look ridiculous. The cutters replied that Hector Millmount was too old. Clarissa Nocton was fifteen years younger than him and they would never be able to make him look like a suitable proposition for her. The arguments continued for an hour and by the time they should have voted, personal insults of a very strong nature were being exchanged at a terrible rate. They even resorted to harsh criticisms of each other's work: the office staff couldn't count figures properly; they were always leaving people short on their salaries and making a mess of the tax deductions; production was forever being halted because of stock shortages caused by inefficient clerical workers. As for the cutters, they should all have had their eyes tested: they couldn't cut a birthday cake properly; the office staff were always dealing with complaints from irate customers complaining that their boxes were too big or small or long; unimaginable sums of money had been wasted because the cutters couldn't arrive in the morning without hangovers and do a decent day's work. With such insults flying they did not get to take a vote before a brawl broke out. In the mêlée the office staff headed straight for Lucha Bellingham, who received a broken jaw. This settled the issue beyond doubt. When my father arrived home he had a blackening eye and a bruise on his forehead and he was fuming about the white-collared fairies who wouldn't fight fair. There was only one thing my mother could do. She went and made some tea. The secret of the Punjab would again settle her nerves and make things seem less critical.

While the cutters and the office were beating hell

out of each other, I was being thrown out of the departure terminal and on to the dangerous streets around the port. As in the case of the letter from Amy, I could not have foreseen that my father would become involved in a fight over the lead role in an amateur operatic production. If there had been some way that I could have been notified of these events then I am certain that I would have returned home and postponed my journey until another time. When it rains it pours, they say, and that day it was pouring for my mother, who was about to experience the greatest trauma of her life. I was thankful as I sat on the deck of the ship that man had discovered tea. I knew it would be a constant friend to her during the time she faced. That and the box-room of her birth.

I never asked her this, but I have a feeling – in the way that you sense things about what people are thinking – that she knew from the moment she realised it was the day of the Great Garlic Harvest, that something seriously wrong was heading her way. My grandfather's defeat in the garlic stakes and her discovery of him rubbing milk into his head, the letter from Amy, the tattered state of my father post opera-wars – these were all connected by an isobar of trouble. I am certain that, as she put ice on his bulging forehead and gentian violet on his cuts, she knew this latest disaster was not to be the final one of the day. It lay revealed as a stretch of time abandoned by God, a black hole from which terrible events emerged. Insanity, crime and injury had already come through it; and the later the evening went on, the more she knew that by the same token that this Monday spewed out trouble, it also sucked in hope. I think she knew before she told anyone or before anyone else even began to suspect it that I had gone without trace. By the time my father had cursed me for being so late she knew that something was wrong. By the time he had progressed to worrying that something was wrong, she had begun to prepare for the worst. And by the time he had begun to prepare himself for the worst, she had resigned herself to the fact that she would not see me again. She was an outrider for others' thoughts, and they arrived at a point long after she had been and gone. That was why she passed through the period of panic so early. She had a feeling that all the efforts it would provoke would be in vain and knew in the way that mothers sometimes do about their children, that I was not to be found.

My father went knocking on all the doors he could find. He scared many people half to death when they opened their doors and found a bandaged, panicked man standing in front of them. He brought the whole neighbourhood out. Women were screaming that it had happened again, that the collective guard had slipped and allowed the body-snatcher to return. Inspector Throckmorton, who had begun to regain respect after the complete failure of his efforts to find Rory Brophy, saw it all happening again. That case had almost led to the break-up of his marriage and a nervous collapse. His wife Crisula had been used to being revered as the spouse of the Chief of Police, but this respect had all evaporated in the weeks and months after Rory's disappearance. 'If I can do my job properly, why can't he do his?' became a catch-phrase. Crisula Throckmorton had heard this taunt a thousand times. Buying groceries in The Anchove, she would hear Gretta Pickering (the owner) say in a low but audible voice, 'If I can do my job properly, why can't he do his?' It was the same with Ermintrude Rowntree in the Post Office and Ignatius Connolly the shoe merchant. They all wanted to know why it was that they could do their jobs properly but the Chief of Police could not do his.

Loyal to his training at the National Academy of Competent Policemen, Inspector Throckmorton arrived at our house after the mandatory period since my last sighting, declared me a missing person and announced that there were three essentials to success-fully concluding a case such as this: a good nose, good intelligence and good luck. He also announced that the chances of success were greater this time. This was because I was older and considered mentally more stable than Rory at the time of his evaporation; and more importantly, because the search would not be constantly side-tracked by the humours of Wino the canine nymphomaniac, who had chased his end once too often and been squashed beneath the wheels of a truck filled with German televisions during 'the case of the missing kitbag'.

There had been a big scandal at the National Aca-demy of Competent Policemen a year previous when an internal investigation into the Dog Unit discovered that Sergeant Billy Whitcombe (the officer-in-charge) had been using his position to develop an illegal but lucrative business as a dog stud-farmer, specialising in German shepherds and labradors. The outcome of this was that the animals emerged after months of 'training' good for nothing but sex. This led to many unfortunate incidents, such as that of Major, the explosives sniffer dog. Two visiting Arab diplomats had been killed by a car bomb only minutes after

Major had 'thoroughly' examined their limousine. Sash the narcotics sniffer dog fared little better. He died in the second week of duty after he ate half a kilo of cocaine disguised as the inside of an ice-hockey helmet. His handlers reported that his death was slow and starry-eyed. The internal investigation revealed that the force was in possession of a pack of useless dogs who were dispatched to a dogs' home, while a clean-up began at their alma mater. It was from this school that Wino had graduated.

The real truth about Inspector Throckmorton's complacency as regards my case, despite his dismal record, had nothing to do with the training he had received at the National Academy of Competent Policemen, nor with the three essentials of finding missing persons nor with the absence of Wino the dog. His complacency stemmed from a source which in fact flew in the face of everything he had been taught and had learnt through his professional career. In the hours after the official declaration of my being missing, Inspector Throckmorton made his way to an area of the city called Velope, where he had an appointment for five in the morning. This appointment had been set without words being exchanged. He had simply dialled a certain number and listened for three dialling tones. He had repeated this four times and then waited for his own phone to ring. He had then counted the number of rings, which told him at what time he should come. It had rung five times, so at four-thirty in the morning the Inspector was walking the streets of Velope.

Velope was an old part of the city which had once been fashionable, but the fine buildings were now inhabited by the poor and the shifty. What had been the University of Very Advanced Studies was now a brothel. Squatters filled the rooms of the nineteenth-century masterpiece by Emmanuel Nolan (architect and polo player), which had been built to mark the defeat of the latter-day neo-post-pro-Gregorians in the ninth and final episode of the Religious Wars. In the old part of this old part of the city, Inspector Throckmorton walked (without uniform, as the police were not popular in Velope) and he came to the street named after Gregory Manella. Half-way along it a plaque on a wall marked the home of this man, who was affectionately known as 'the Unfortunate Scientist'. Legend had it that Gregory Manella was sitting in the front room of his house and looking across the narrow street when he saw a woman open an upstairs window and dump a bucket of human wastage down on to the pavement. This was a common practice in those days, but it set Gregory's mind to work. Why, he wondered, did the human wastage fall down and not up or sideways? This incident proved the genesis of fifteen years' work which culminated when he produced his findings in 1688, which was one year after Newton and the reason why Gregory Manella became known as the Unfortunate Scientist. The world had forgotten him, and only a fading plaque on the wall marked the spot where his futile investigations were first inspired.

The very room where Gregory Manella had looked out and seen human wastage tumbling to earth was now the studio of a woman by the name of Monica Bedfield, known as the 'Queen of Rats'. When she was an infant, Monica had spent her days wandering beneath the streets in the sewers, which held a special fascination for her. She seemed to be attracted by the tranquillity of the place. 'It was like being in the countryside,' she would say. 'There is such peace down there, and the sound of running water, like a stream.' She got away from the madness of the world which raged above her head by descending through a manhole near where she lived. There she had spent her days – no, her childhood years – without seeming to suffer for it. Her skin was pale from the lack of sunlight, but she was immune from the disease carried by the rodents who shared her adopted habitat.

It was during these formative years that she developed her extraordinary affinity with rats. She learnt to communicate with them. They liked her and often brought her things: small pieces of jewellery they had stolen, keys and ornaments, clothes scavenged from dumps. They brought her things she could wear and which made her beautiful. She would emerge from the manhole in the evenings wearing earrings and watches, carrying handfuls of keys which jangled in the dark, and this was how she became known as the Queen of Rats. Then people began to come to her when they had lost precious and sacred things. On many occasions it was the rats who had taken them, and she would return them without complaint or embarrassment. She came to know each rodent individually and could identify the parts of the city where they scavenged. This was how she had been instrumental in the detection of a kidnapped infant whose parents had come to her after receiving a ransom note demanding a sum of money exceeding everything they owned. The Queen of Rats went into the sewers and returned the following evening with a tiny white sock with the initials DD on it, which was identified as belonging to the missing infant. The sock had been brought to her by a rat which hunted in the disused power station at Briggan. The building was surrounded by police, who rescued the child and arrested two brothers and a third accomplice, all of whom were given fifteen years' hard labour.

The Queen of Rats was not officially recognised by the police because they did not want to be seen wearing out a path to her door to ask her assistance in solving cases they had failed to close. But it was common knowledge that many of the people who went to her were members of the force anxious to see their detection-rate improve. Many a promotion was due to her intervention, and she charged heavily for her services. Inspector Throckmorton had resisted the temptation to call on her for as long as he could, but he saw himself being left behind by fellow officers whose detection-rates surpassed his own. His belief that her talents were a temporary fluke showed no signs of being vindicated, and he had already begun to seek her help with lesser crimes. My disappearance was an opportunity for him to solve an important case which would attract the attention of his senior officers and rebuild his reputation, and so it was that just before five in the morning he knocked on the door of the house where Gregory Manella had noticed some shit fall to earth.

Inspector Throckmorton gave the woman a list of the things I had been wearing when I was last seen. He also told her of the watch I wore on my wrist and the miraculous medal of Saint Damien the Plumber which had been given to me by my grandmother on the day I first swallowed the Body of Christ. She told him that she would do what she could and that he should return in two days at the same time. When he left, the Queen went into the sewers and sent the rats to look for me. The following evening she returned and sat on an armchair she had placed at the confluence of five tunnels, and the rats came to her all evening, one of them bearing the miraculous medal of Saint Damien the Plumber. She passed it on to the Inspector with the news that it had been returned by one of the rats and gave him the precise location where this rodent liked to scavenge. The Chief of Police returned to his station a very happy man, believing that he would soon be the hero of the hour. He put on his uniform, drove to the port and found the smelly lane with large warehouse doors on one side and the back wall of a coal depot on the other. The Queen of Rats had told him to go to the far end of the lane. The rat who had found the medal dared not venture up to the street where it was busy and the deck-chair hawkers left scraps of meat with crushed glass in them. He went to the far end and saw a body perched up on the ledge before a warehouse door. He put his hand on the shoulder of the body and called my name. But it wasn't me – I was on the high seas by then. The body that lay on the ledge was the African-on-the-Run, who was taken to the police station. There, a large angry crowd had gathered at the news that a man had been arrested and was about to be charged with kidnapping.

People tend not to believe tramps and the Inspector was adamant that the African-on-the-Run had kidnapped me, and knew where I was and if I was alive or dead. The African was regretting his petty crime, the stealing of my medal from around my neck as I slept. But that was all he knew, he pleaded. My grandfather interrupted the insulation of his brain when he heard the news that they had arrested somebody. He had to be restrained by a number of officers in the police station, who pushed him back outside. He then pounded on the door and threatened to tear the prisoner's head off with his hands. My father was so distraught at the possibility that the suspect might announce at any moment that he had murdered me and chopped me into small pieces that he was taken ill and had to be sedated by a doctor. My mother knew the man was innocent. She told the Inspector this when she verified that the medal was mine and then she slipped away to the room where she was born, from where she could sense that I was far away and getting further all the time.

What followed was a sustained period of tea-making which had no equal. Inspector Throckmorton came out the front door of the police station and told the crowd to go home because there would be no announcements that day. These things took time. Interrogation in such cases had to be meticulous to avoid a miscarriage of justice. The crowd hissed and booed and my grandfather still insisted that he wanted to tear the prisoner's head off. (You must remember that I am unaware that any of this is happening. It was yet another unforeseeable consequence of my vanishing.)

I don't want to jump the gun too much by telling you the outcome of the Inspector's questioning, but suffice it to say that the African-on-the-Run was sorely regretting his ever meeting me. If he got out of this (I am being as cautious as I can here) he would most certainly never engage in crime again. All his troubles had been for the sake of a worthless piece of pewter with a tiny patch of blood-stained linen in the centre (there were thousands of these medals available and I can only hazard a guess that there must have been a bloodbath when they were all made). The African-on-the-Run now faced the possibility of a life of hard labour in prison. In fact, it was not the prospect of being incarcerated for the rest of his life which frightened him so much as the notion that he would have to work through it. This upset him so much that he did not even think of the usual fate of those found guilty of crimes against children (even though I was eighteen, Rory had been three years younger when he vanished and the African would have to answer for that as well). Very few such criminals ever finished their sentences. They had to be kept in solitary confinement for their own safety, but it never proved possible to protect them at all times. Doors were always mysteriously left open, they were always gotten too. This never occurred to him as he sat in the police cell and rued the moment he had been attracted to the object hanging round my neck. I will tell you the outcome of his ordeal shortly, but for now the Inspector is dispersing the crowd outside his station. This was the signal for the mass putting-on of kettles.

As well as being a panacea for problems and a toast at celebrations, tea was also the ideal beverage for homecoming. Whenever people arrived back from the city or from church or work, their instinctive reaction was always to reach for their kettles. It was as much part of coming home as taking off their coats and putting on their slippers. Now there were dozens of them arriving home simultaneously and within minutes the street rang to the whistles of boiling water. By the time everyone else had arrived back, my mother had already drunk four cups of it. She sat in the room where she was born and watched her father come up the street, miming his words of abuse and going through the motions of pulling someone's head off with his bare hands. He was muttering furiously to himself and seemed very upset. He was the only one who did not seek the comfort of the brew. No longer for him the restrained sipping of tea. This required something more violent, so he reboiled his milk and began again to massage his head.

This did not trouble my mother as it had done before. She sat with the ease of a woman who has had everything put into perspective. She knew I was alive and well, and also that things had changed irrevocably. Senile dementia and bar-room brawls were all just part of the same process which had taken me away. There was no point in getting upset at the course of God's events.

When she returned to our house from the room she was born, my mother sat quietly amongst the red-hot tempers of the people around her. There were ten or eleven of them there, who commiserated with her and told her that the whole thing would be over soon. She should not worry. She should relax and have a cup of tea. During this tea group (psychologists must forgive the pun), all sorts of theories and stories emerged. Lodged on the couch between Billy McCauley, the professional drummer who could not pass any object without tapping on it, and Millicent Eviston, the tax evader, in between both of these sat, no perched, Maude Tennison, the Mother of Morons. She had had eleven or twelve different offspring by that stage, one as thick as the next. Maude Tennison began to explain her theory which she based on the books of Professor Nathaniel Ormrod, the 'noted psychologist' as she called him. Quite what he was 'noted' for she never said, but on the basis of her ideas he should have been noted for his stupidity. My case, she said, was proof positive of his hypothesis concerning the generation gap. I was an only child who believed that the genes of his parents had conspired against him to cast him in the role of loner, a victim of the practice of hysterectomy, who felt obliged when he reached adulthood to set off in search of the companionship denied him by the surgeon when he removed the womb. Professor Nathaniel Ormrod would have diagnosed that the real motivation behind my disappearance was a subconscious search for that womb, a longing to find it and climb back inside, a desire to return to the days before I was born, when the integrity of my mother's organs still held out the promise that I would have brothers and sisters to accompany me in my life.

These were the things this woman spoke about: the crackpot theories of this professor, which had been proved right on many occasions by her own children. This was the greatest insult she ever paid me. I was now being compared with the Tennisons. The correspondence between my behaviour and theirs was being highlighted. They had disappeared many times, and so we were all alike. The Tennisons and I were birds of a feather. What she failed to point out, and what I must make clear, is that their disappearances involved no premeditation. Premeditation requires the ability to assess a situation as being unsatisfactory and to decide on a course of action to remedy it. This was beyond them. The Tennisons did not disappear in the wake of premeditation, they simply got lost. They were so stupid that they wandered off the routes they knew and couldn't find their way.

While Maude Tennison continued to slander me by association, Inspector Throckmorton tried in vain to get the African-on-the-Run to confess to my abduction. He insisted he had never seen the miraculous medal of Saint Damien the Plumber before. He was too old and weak to abduct an eighteen-year-old boy. How could he possibly have managed to do that? He was always being chased by people of that age. The twelve-year-old son of a deck-chair hawker had beaten him up a week previous. A boy, a youngster only two-thirds my age, had beaten him up, and now he was being accused of abducting and murdering me. The Inspector was beginning to see the frailty of his case. Could he possibly stand up in court with the miraculous medal of Saint Damien the Plumber and base his case against the accused on the fact that it had been given to him by a woman who claimed to be able to converse with rats and who told him that she knew for a fact that the rodent who brought her the medal was the one that scavenged at the bottom of the alleys near the port? This was the only connection that there was between the African-on-the-Run and the medal – the word of a woman who heard it from a rat. The Inspector could hear the howls of laughter from the public gallery. He could see the numbed faces of the jury, their inability to believe what they were hearing. He could imagine the anger of the judge, who would fume that in all his life he had never heard such nonsense. The case would be dismissed.

The African-on-the-Run denied everything. He did not recognise my picture. It was a natural instinct for survival, but he said 'No' to everything, and when the mandatory period of custody had elapsed, the Inspector was forced to release him.

5   *The Paluxy River Theory*

In 1938, the fishermen working out of a port in South Africa caught an unusual fish which they had not seen before. The specimen aroused the attention of the curator of a local museum, a woman by the name of Miss Courtney-Latimer. Miss Courtney-Latimer wrote to Professor J.B.L. Smith of Grahamstown University describing the fish in detail. By the time Professor Smith got to see the fish, its innards had decomposed and been thrown away, but he recognised it as a coelacanth. What was so unusual about this was that the coelacanth was presumed to have been extinct for seventy million years. Professor Smith, a leading authority on fish, was beside himself with excitement. Such was the extent of his happiness that he named the specimen Latimeria after the museum curator who first brought it to his attention. The discovery was hailed as the scientific event of the century and a massive hunt was set in motion to find another live specimen of the newly named Latimeria. Pictures of the fish were circulated to all the fishing villages along the south and eastern coasts of South Africa and a large reward was offered to the person who would find another specimen.

145

The search was in vain for fifteen years. Then the fishermen of the Comorra Islands in the Indian Ocean got wind of the excitement about the fish and told everyone that they saw this fish regularly, and that the one found off South Africa must have strayed from its natural waters. The coelacanth, or Latimeria, was significant in another way: it was the fish which, some 350 million years ago, had first climbed out of the sea on to land. This was why Professor J.B.L. Smith of Grahamstown University had recognised it immediately and been so overcome with joy that he named a fish after a woman and offered money to any trawlerman who would bring him another one.

Whatever it was that drove the coelacanth to crawl out of the water and explore the shoreline, no one will ever know; but it proved a turning-point in evolution, for the backbone that ran down that particular fish's back was the first to cross dry land. In the course of time the fish's pectoral fins became legs and it stood up and walked; and, over some 150 million years, a fish became a dinosaur. The rest, as they could say, is natural history. This was what the fishermen had found: the fish with the exploratory instinct which changed the world. The reptilian generations which came millions of years after this vertebrate had first bashed itself against the rocks and died in the name of evolution ruled the earth. They also liked America. They were particularly fond of North America – the south-west to be more precise. To be more precise again, the dinosaurs loved Texas. Perhaps this is where the people of the Lone Star State get their love of things which are big. There must be something in the air, an odour from the Permian age 280 million years ago, the musk of dinosaurs still lingering in the atmosphere. It was to Texas that the great reptiles came in vast numbers, and it was in Texas that they died. When their time was up, they faced extinction in the company of others. There was no slinking off alone, no such solitary deaths for the Texas dinosaurs.

The River Brazos rises in New Mexico but doesn't reach anything like mature riverhood until it has crossed the state line into Texas. It flows in a south-easterly direction across Texas and enters the Gulf of Mexico near Galveston. The River Brazos is not what concerns us. It is the Paluxy, a tributary of the Brazos, which is of importance – in particular, the ancient history of the Paluxy. If Texas is famous for the quantity of dinosaur remains found there, the Paluxy River is especially spectacular in this respect. The remains of thirty dinosaurs, of fourteen different species, have been found near it, which is why it was chosen for the construction of the National Dinosaur Monument. This is all very exciting for natural historians and palaeontologists, but it is not these remains which concern us either.

You may be forgiven for thinking at this point that the printer has made some terrible mistake. Perhaps it was his wedding anniversary the day before he printed this book and he had such a hangover that he inadvertently mixed up two books: a fictional novel and a textbook for natural history students. Perhaps you will never know the ending of my story, and will have to make a guess while you read about dinosaur remains and Texan rivers. What of the natural history students? If they are as penniless as others, what a shock they will get when they open their hard-earned acquisition to find nothing about their chosen subject until now. What a travesty! But let me put your mind at rest. There has been no mix-up, nor have I become bored with my story and decided to try my hand at writing about old bones. None of these things has happened. This is still my story and I am on a boat to Sweden; but do bear in mind the brief account I have given of the River Brazos and its tributary, the Paluxy, which flow through Texas and have been the site of major palaeontological finds. The relevance of these facts will become evident – I mention them now by way of preparing you.

As the first day of the boat journey passed I laid to rest one of my biggest fears: the one which had me draped over the railings so that my backside would become more familiar to my fellow passengers than my face; the fear which had them calling me 'pasty face' and the floor of the dining car covered in small molehills of sawdust where I had vomited after dinner. I was pleasantly surprised at how well my stomach behaved. This gave me the confidence to strut about the deck like a seasoned veteran of the high seas. I left it to the others to abuse the dolphins who came alongside the ship as ambassadors of the underworld only to have their heads vomited upon by queasy-bellied novices. Not for me such pollution of the oceans. I felt I was born to sail and observed the other passengers with a degree of superiority. They were a particularly unspectacular lot. Most of them were middle aged and I was surprised at how few children there were. Of them all there was only one who seemed interesting to me. You will have noticed that I have a penchant for nicknames, and to this passenger I pinned the label 'The Clicker', because of his habit of clicking his fingers at people to attract their attention. Mostly he used it when calling a woman who I presumed to be his wife, because they were both too old to be illicit lovers.

'The Clicker' was tall, well-built and bald. When he wasn't clicking his fingers, he was playing cards. He spoke to everybody (except his wife) and sat like the King of England at a small round table in the bar of the ship, clicking his fingers at people to invite them to come and play cards with him. He had many things to say and liked drinking a clear liquid, which I guessed to be gin or vodka. When people did accept his offer he insisted on buying them a drink. This was when his clicking proved handiest. The woman I presumed to be his wife never stayed with him at the table. She sat on one of the long benches by the wall behind him where she read her books. When he clicked his fingers in the air above his right shoulder, she came to him and he would despatch her to the bar to buy drinks for his fellow players and himself. As well as being a good talker, he was also a very good card-player. He had to be, to be as old as he was and still playing. A bad card-player would have given up years before, or been sent to prison at the insistence of their creditors. The rate at which he bought drinks and the size of the stakes he gambled gave him away as a man who was not short of money. He clicked his fingers at me a number of times, but I played deaf as I had no intention of gambling away my meagre wealth with such a sharp. It was only in the afternoons that I would see him. He never appeared until three o'clock, but his wife would still go into the bar and sit on the long bench to read her book.

It was on the third day of the trip that 'The Clicker' got me. I was sitting at a table on the deck when he came and sat down beside me. He had a glass of his clear liquid with him, and when he joined me he did so with the confidence of a man who had known me all my life. He introduced himself as Erno Wellbeloved, adding that perhaps I knew him as Denis Frankl. I told him that I had no desire to be rude but I knew him as neither. He laughed a huge laugh and drank some of his liquid. He told me he was sixty-two and said he was enormously happy with life. I asked him why I should know him as Denis Frankl and he said that that was his *nom de plume*. He was Denis Frankl the author of westerns, of which he had written seventy-two, but I was not a great fan of western films and certainly not of western books. This was perfectly acceptable to him, he assured me (insisting that I call him Erno), but was I as set against playing cards as reading the sort of books he wrote? I told him I was, especially when the invitation came from someone who played as well as he did. I had been watching him in the last few days and there were many passengers who had lost much of their spending money to his skill.

Erno Wellbeloved told me the reason for his happiness. I mentioned to him that I never saw him in the mornings and he explained that he did all his writing at that time of day. He would begin at nine o'clock and work for six hours, taking half-an-hour break at half past twelve for lunch. It was not the quality of his writing which made him happy. The likes of 'Sunset at White Deer' and 'The Man with the Scar on his Heart' were not among the great novels of the century. Nor was it the money that his writing brought him; and he did live well. It was surprising how much people could earn from churning out such drivel (his words, not mine). The reason for his happiness was something which went much deeper and . . . I have to admit, it surprised me that a man who played cards for big money and felt no remorse at seeing his opponents leave the table in great distress, who wrote rubbishy novels about a world that never existed and, most of all, who clicked his fingers at his wife (he confirmed that they were married, but that he no longer felt any love for her) – it surprised me that such a man possessed the sensitivity to be happy for the reason he explained to me.

His happiness stemmed from the plight of Warren Solerno. You may well ask, who is Warren Solerno? I certainly did. I said, 'Who is Warren Solerno?' The instant that these words had exited my mouth, in fact the precise moment the morpheme 'er' passed my teeth, Erno Wellbeloved's face became contorted with such an expression as to convince me that I had said something particularly terrible. I quickly retraced my way through the sentence I had just uttered, sure that the villain of the piece must be in there somewhere. Before I had begun the sentence, myself and Erno were getting on quite well, despite having nothing in common except our gender and being fellow passengers on a ferry to Sweden. Yes indeed, the culprit which had elicited such an expression on Erno's face (still fixed in a gaze of ghastly incredulity) was somewhere within the confines of the sentence 'Who is Warren Solerno?' I was in that position, always difficult to handle, when you feel that you have revealed a real ignorance about yourself, but you are unsure as to what you are ignorant of. I can only say that I was very much aware that my ignorance of Warren Solerno came as a great shock to Erno Wellbeloved. After some considerable amount of gasping and brow-wiping (all of which struck me as melo-dramatic in the extreme), Erno's face returned to something approaching normality. Then, clenching his fist so it beat out every syllable he uttered, he told me that Warren Solerno was the greatest writer in history.

I felt a little more relaxed on hearing this because I believe that Warren Solerno must be the real name of a writer better known by his *nom de plume*. I confessed that my knowledge of literature was not all that it could be and certainly did not extend to knowledge of the real names of the great writers. I knew that Samuel Langhorne Clemens was Mark Twain (this was one of the little titbits of information I had memorised to impress Rory Brophy with my knowledge of literature). A name like Warren Solerno could surely not have been the real name of a Russian writer. Shakespeare too seemed unlikely, as did Dickens. Solerno sounded Hispanic, so I tried Cervantes but without success. Perhaps he was American, Steinbeck maybe, or Hemingway. But not these either, so I gave up. I was being shown up as a fraud – in the past I had pretended to be so clever on the subject, but now the chickens were coming home to roost. I had met my match. I was going to be caught out because I did not know the real name of the greatest writer in the world was Warren Solerno.

Accepting my defeat I lay back in my seat and prepared for humiliation. 'Tell me, then,' I said, 'who is Warren Solerno?' Erno Wellbeloved answered me that Warren Solerno was Warren Solerno. But he was supposed to be the greatest writer of all time . . . I admitted (now) to being no authority on literature but

I was not so ignorant as not to have heard of so great an author. So who was this Warren Solerno, I asked again. Erno Wellbeloved told me that Warren Solerno was the son of Dimitri Solerno and Marianna Florence. They lived in a small fishing village in the Dominican Republic. As a child, Dimitri Solerno was interested in two things: running and sex. He was a fast runner, and spent much of the first thirteen years of his life running everywhere. Up and down the steep hills of the town he would go, stopping at either the sea or the top of the hill on which the town was built. The villagers had to be careful when he was running or he would knock them over. All they could ever say about him was, 'Here comes Dimitri' or 'There goes Dimitri.' When he reached the age of puberty, Dimitri's second interest began to increase in importance. He was not a complete novice – he used to tell his friends that he could remember being born and seeing his mother's tush. He was also very fond of looking at the women's underthings hanging on the clothes lines which he ran past. Even as a boy, the huge underwear of some of the fat ladies held a real fascination for him.

When he was fourteen the changes which took place inside him allowed him to act on his second interest. One evening he left the house after dinner and set off on his evening run. Taking such exercise after a meal held no problems for him. His intestines were used to it and had evolved accordingly so they processed the food very quickly. It was true that Dimitri had the fastest intestines in the whole Dominican Republic. When he reached the top of the hill on which the town stood, he turned and began his descent. Whether it was the way he had his trousers on or not, he began to experience a wonderful sensation inside them and he knew that something quite terrific was happening. This was better than the tingling feeling he had had before. (And the truth about his running was that he did it because of the sensation he got when his mickey rubbed against his trousers. It was difficult to get it in the right place and sometimes he had to run for hours, constantly readjusting his clam-digger by poking his hand into his seamless left pocket. But it was all worth it for the moments of pleasure he would feel before his weapon slipped out of position again.) But this evening, as Dimitri Solerno turned at the top of the hill and began his descent, he could immediately feel that everything had clicked (or slipped) into place. His lucky stars were with him, the planetary alignments were favourable.

Running down through the streets the sensation was seminal. The super-fit Dimitri started to gasp for breath. The faster he ran the greater the sensation. He knew he was heading for something big. He reached speeds that were positively dangerous in such a con-fined area, and almost killed Grandma Le Guin when she stepped out of her front door for a good spit. He knocked over baskets and tables, dogs and cats ran for their lives, and a trail of disaster was left behind him as if a tornado had swept through the town – Hurricane Dimitri. The big thing was about to happen, but he was running out of street and getting very close to the sea . . . . But it happened just in time. Something exploded in his trousers right outside his house, whence his mother saw him flash by screaming 'Jesus, Jesus, Jesus . . . . Oh Mama Jesus.' He managed to stop just at the waterfront and bent over to rest his hands on his knees. When he looked at his trousers there was a large wet stain around his pelvis. 'Oh my God,' he thought to himself, 'I've pissed myself with excitement.'

Dimitri Solerno had discovered the truth about sex. This was why men chased women, he thought. From that day on he began to chase girls everywhere so that he could have sex by experiencing that remarkable explosion in his pants which made him urinate. It became problematical for him because the fathers of the girls told him to cut it out or face the consequences. It was Marianna Florence who saved him when she told him he could chase her whenever he wished. One day she was walking home after taking dried fish to her sister's house when she heard her name being called out. She looked behind to see Dimitri running down the hill at terrible speed with the look of a gangster on his face. He chased her up a side alley which ran out before the explosion occurred in his trousers. He was riddled with angst. When Marianna asked him why he was standing there like a scolded child, he told her that he had failed to have sex with her because the lane was too short. Her roars of laughter dried the clothes on the lines. There and then, she ended his innocence and his ignorance, and that was how Warren Solerno was conceived at the bottom of the lane after a long run.

Those were the better days, before the fascists perfected the art of wiping out large sections of the population. The fascists were quite stupid. On a rumour that a man who had tried to assassinate a deputy-head fascist by dropping a piano on to his car was hiding in Warren Solerno's town, the fascists killed the entire adult male population. Dimitri Solerno was killed doing what he did best – running.

They shot him in the back, the bullet severing his spine so he didn't die immediately but two months afterwards, when he realised he would never run again. This took place when Warren Solerno was thirteen. His mother said to him that he must bear witness to what had happened to the men, especially to his father. 'If his bones lie in the earth for a million years and turn to fossils, somebody, someday might find them and the bones will show the evidence that Dimitri Solerno was shot in the back,' she said.

Warren Solerno was entrusted by his mother with the duty of avenging the death of his father and the men of the town. Like most of the children who had seen the massacre, Warren did not need to be told that such a deed had to be avenged. As they grew up in the village, the children plotted how they would return to the fascists the pain which had stained their youth. Most of them chose to join the communist insurgents who lived in the mountains. But one, instead, set about eating the banana and pineapple crops of the big farmers who supported the fascists. This man was the legendary Anto 'the Belly' Borgia. At thirty-four stones he was too fat to fight, so he attacked the fascists in their pockets by devouring large portions of the farm produce which financed them. He laid waste whole areas like a plague of locusts and claimed that he would eat the enemy into submission. The energies of the insurgents, meanwhile, were directed towards blowing up bridges and arranging the ambush of government troops. Most of the fatherless children decided that this was where their future lay. But not Warren Solerno. He decided that he would avenge the deaths by writing of the atrocity and exposing the enemy for what it really was.

156

The urge to write had always been with him, but it never before seemed quite so necessary. His ambition, however, was thwarted by circumstances. Each time he sat down to write, his mother would say to him that he should go and catch fish or they would starve, or go and fetch water or they would die of thirst. Even at night, when everything was dark and he sat by a paraffin lamp, he was forever interrupted by the nightmares of his mother, who kept having visions of the moment when her husband ran for the last time. Warren Solerno's living conditions made it very difficult for him to release on to paper the ideas that threatened to suffocate him. There were remarkable conspiracies of events and objects to deny him. On one of the few nights when his mother's sleep was uninterrupted, Warren began to write of his father's love of running. The words came easily to him, over the edge of his brain and tumbling down through his right arm and hand on to the page. He wrote superb prose for an hour before a mosquito entered his room and hovered near the inkwell. Without thinking about what he was doing, Warren flicked his hand to despatch the insect but knocked over the bottle of precious liquid. He had no more in his house and it was the early hours of the morning. He ran to the shop of Constance Biscuit to fetch some more before the source of his inspiration dried up. But Constance wasn't home – she had gone to the wedding of her fifteen-year-old niece to the illegitimate son of an illegitimate woman, who had gained respect for himself by his exploits in business. The relative empire he had created based on salsify had brought him considerable wealth and the honourable nickname of 'The Brilliant Bastard'. Warren was only prevented from

157

kicking down the door of the shop by the thought that he might end up in jail, where he would certainly not be able to write. He returned to his house and in the kitchen tried to concoct a liquid mixture which could be substituted for ink. He tried to write with coffee. Then he mixed vinegar in it and added cornflower to thicken it. Boiled green peppers and potatoes were also tried, but to no avail. He even added some of his own blood to a little water and flour, but nothing would work. He extinguished the paraffin lamp and went to bed a frustrated man.

These were the kinds of things which happened to Warren Solerno when he tried to write his book. There were other travesties too. The time three chickens got into his room and tore his paper to pieces. The day the pig stuck its head in his window and swallowed the box containing his nibs, dying a slow and painful death. With such things happening all the time, it became very difficult for him to continue to justify his decision not to join the rebels in the mountains. People would say to him, 'How come you are not fighting to avenge your father's death?' He would answer that he would avenge it all right, but that there were more memorable ways of doing it than killing an isolated fascist soldier in the dense forest at night. 'Then where is this great book of yours?' they would ask him. 'It's mostly in my head still,' he could only answer. They began calling him a coward and jeered that this book thing was nothing but an excuse. The real reason he wouldn't go and fight was because he was afraid. His mother became his biggest critic. She told him he was a disgrace to his father and shamed the name of Solerno. She told him he had carrot juice in his veins. But despite the criticisms, Warren Solerno continued to try to write the novel that would change the way the world saw his country.

It was an agonisingly slow process, as intractable as the war itself. He constantly revised and rewrote. He was half-way through his third chapter when his mother died of a heart attack in the middle of one of her nightmares. This was the release he had been waiting for. In the months after her death, the gods looked favourably on his task. He entered a period of sustained output. The animals stayed out of his room, even the mosquitoes observed a curfew. There were no more weddings to interrupt his supply of materials and the greatest novel in history began to emerge.

In the hills above the town the war began to go well for the insurgents, despite the death of Anto 'the Belly' Borgia from an inflammation of the intestine due to ridiculous gluttony. The fascists' days were all but numbered and they retreated to the capital where they were encircled. There was no harbour to offer them an exit. The President disappeared one night, only to be uncovered three days later trying to walk out of the city disguised as an old woman with 15 million dollars' worth of jewellery hidden in a sack of flour on his back. This was the end of the war. The fascist troops deserted their regiments and many were murdered pleading reasons for doing what they had done. Warren Solerno's town went wild when the insurgents returned from the mountains. They drank and sang the songs they had composed during the war. In the early hours of the morning some of them went and burned down the house of Warren Solerno the coward. He died with his almost-finished master-piece, screaming that he was on their side and that his book would be the greatest tirade against oppression the world had ever seen. He was on their side he shouted, he was on their side. But that was the end of Warren Solerno – the greatest writer in history.

Erno Wellbeloved sat back in his chair and put his hands behind his head. His belly stuck out so his navel could be seen and I noticed a clump of hair growing out of it. He had a big smile on his face that said 'QED' to me. It was clear from his posture that it was my turn to speak. I knew he was playing with me, that I was his favourite toy of the moment. I could sense in a way that I was supposed to be annoyed and debated whether to stand up and walk away; or better still, whether I should tell him to take his silly stories elsewhere. After all, he was the one who had come over to me. No invitation had been issued, and maybe it was time to remind him of that. But I thought that might be the ignorant thing to do. It would be a clear admission that I felt intellectually intimidated by him. It would not be much better than hitting him in the face and claiming to be his superior for it. While I pondered what to do, he raised his right hand above his shoulder and clicked his fingers. His wife came up behind him. I was astonished. How had he known she was there? We were outside on deck and she was behind him. Her soft shoes had made no sound and she hadn't spoken, yet he had known she would be there and had called her to him like you would a dog. (Later he explained that he had smelt the very expensive perfume which she insisted he buy for her.) Without even looking at her, in fact looking straight at me, he spoke in a low voice sending her to the bar to buy two drinks. So it was there on the deck, in the wake of a silly story, that I was handed my first chalice of alcohol.

When I finally enquired as to what this w
Warren Solerno business was, Erno Wellbelo
laughed the laugh of a satisfied man. He had found
himself the one passenger on every voyage who
would sit and listen to his stories, and that was me. I
was giving him more pleasure than all the card-
players who had systematically handed their money
over to him. He was happy because I had entered into
the reason for his existence. It was simple, he told me.
Warren Solerno was a fictitious character who represented the great men and women of history who had
never reached the peak of their brilliance for whatever
reason. The painters who had never painted. The
musicians who had never composed. The mathemati-
cians who had never added numbers and would
never be remembered. But not Erno Wellbeloved. He
had discovered, while standing two feet away from a
Rembrandt at the National Academy of Artistic
Endeavours, what the secret of his life was. He peered
at one brush stroke, one tiny jab of the artist's hand on
the face of his portrait. He stood in relation to the
painting exactly where Rembrandt himself had stood
hundreds of years before and reached out his hand to
add a stroke to his canvas. Erno Wellbeloved now
stood and stared at that very same stroke. It was then,
in the company of the works of great people, that the
only reason for being alive presented itself to him. He
ran from the gallery with a speed which startled the
guards, who thought that anyone running that fast
through their halls must have stolen something. Five
of them pursued him, the train of running men weav-
ing its way along the corridors and out into the
gardens. The guards shouted to one another, 'Why are
you chasing him?' but none of them seemed to know.

When they caught him near the gates, they asked him why he was running. He replied that it was quicker than walking and that he was in a hurry.

He returned to his office above a bakery famed for its perfect boxty pancakes, where he had the job of keeping a record of all the freight containers that entered or left the country. When one came in, he moved its card into the 'In' box. When it left, he moved the card back into the 'Out' box. Erno went into his employer's office and told him that he would be leaving his job a week from that day. The startled man pointed out that he had a wonderful future in the business. The world was just waking up to the possibilities of containers. The technology was improving all the time. New standards were being set. They were even refrigerating them. Great things were happening in the world of containers . . . Erno Wellbeloved could play an important part in that process, yet he was prepared to throw all that away.

Erno arrived home that evening and went into the small bedroom of his house which he used as a storeroom. Within hours he had transformed it into a study and christened it the 'Headroom'. On the first day of his unemployment he went into the Headroom at nine in the morning and began to write 'Has Anyone Seen Jack Wallace?' which he completed in two weeks. He sent it to a publisher who returned it with an unflattering opinion. Erno was undeterred. He wrote a second one called 'Stranger in a Poncho' which he sent to a different publisher who said it needed some work but he would accept it. Since then, Erno Wellbeloved had spent much of the next twenty-five years in the Headroom, where he produced these stories at the rate of one every month or so. He was invited to make appearances and speeches and it was at one of these that he had met his wife, who was the Secretary of the Luttut Western Enthusiasts Club.

Erno Wellbeloved had already told me that he did not love his wife and that the majority of their contact took place across his right shoulder. But she was not stupid, despite her behaviour. Some of his best books had been her ideas. She would read what he had written at the end of each day, then come to him afterwards and stand behind his shoulder and whisper an idea into his ear. 'The Blind Gaucho' had been her creation. It was the story of a blind child who grew up to be an ace gunfighter by timing the draw and aiming his gun by the sound of his opponent's weapon scraping against the holster leather as it was drawn. The Blind Gaucho could track at night by listening for the sound of burning wood and snores in the desert. A legend without eyes, he had died in a duel against a man with a fur-lined holster, but he had been created in a conversation which took place over Erno's right shoulder and went to prove that his wife was not a stupid woman. All this is not to say that he believed what he wrote was of great quality. Perhaps it added in some way to the value of the world, but it was meagre by comparison with the contribution of Rembrandt's painting. Erno Wellbeloved's ambition was not to be regarded in the same light as such a genius, it was simply to be remembered by leaving something behind, so that when people saw it they would know that a man called Erno Wellbeloved had existed at a particular time in history. This was the thought that had struck him as he peered at the artist's brush-stroke: the idea that the movement of Rembrandt's hand, hundreds of years ago, had been carved in time. The ideas that came to Erno Wellbe-loved when he wrote were not brilliant ones, but they would still be there, and every time someone read them, he would be resurrected again – just as he had resurrected Rembrandt when he stood in the National Academy of Artistic Endeavours. Erno went on to tell me that there was a river in Texas called the Brazos which flowed south-eastwards into the Gulf of Mex-ico. It had a tributary called the Paluxy. Millions of years ago a theropod walked across the muddy bank of the Paluxy when the water level was low and left some footprints which can still be seen today. He gave me a copy of his latest book, which he signed, and before he left he asked me again if I played cards. I said, 'No.'

The next morning I sat on my own in the bar of the ship. I felt less intimidated by the smell of alcohol now that I had drunk some of it with Erno. I had only had one glass of his clear liquid, mind you, and I still did not know what it was. That morning I felt depressed as the full extent of what I was doing began to rise up in front of me. I was out of my depth; this sort of thing really wasn't me. My background was far too humble for me to be able to tackle the problem I had set myself.

I went up to the bar, sat on a stool and asked for a glass of 'the clear stuff'. I thought this was quite clever because it both concealed the fact that I did not know what the 'clear stuff' was called, and also sounded like the pet-name that a hardened drinker would have for his favourite beverage. But the barman wasn't having any of it and he dismissed me for being too young. He was perfectly reasonable about it, and even apolo-gised, but my depression was enlarged by this rejection. I went outside and sat on one of the benches for a while before a hand came over my right shoulder with a glass of 'the clear stuff' in it. Erno Wellbeloved's wife came around – in a position I thought she never took up in the company of males. She told me that as it was morning Erno was at his desk, and that she had already passed one or two ideas over his clavicle that day. I asked her if she did not mind that he was given the credit for ideas which were hers, but she said that this was no problem for her as she did not share her husband's obsession with the footprints of dinosaurs. Her name was Elvira Poxon and she was the grand-daughter of Oscar Poxon, the accordion player who boasted that no couple at whose wedding he had performed had ever divorced. When their marriages went through difficult times, people would say to them, 'How can you be so unhappy when you were married to the strains of Oscar Poxon's accordion playing? How can love legalised in the presence of such music ever die?' Oscar Poxon himself had a daughter named Magdalene who hated the sound of the accordion and got married three years before her divorce to Kevin Erasmus, but not before a daughter had been born. This was Elvira Poxon, who grew up in a house with her mother and grandfather, who always said it was a mistake not to have played at his own daughter's wedding. If he had, his granddaughter would not have grown up without her father.

In the Colonial War, Elvira Poxon fought in the Western Command, where she met Billy Cashin. They were married during a half-hour break she had from her duties as an interpreter, with an intelligence officer, whose name they did not know, as the witness. At the end of the war, when the cease-fire terms were announced on the radio by Colonel Wallace P. Prendergast, Billy Cashin was beside himself with anger at what he saw as a betrayal. He stormed from the house where he heard it and beat up an unfortunate beggar who asked him for money, before running up into the mountains where he cried for nine days with such relentlessness that the rivers swelled up and irrigated the vineyards, which gave up a crop of tear-shaped grapes in the summer. When he came down, Billy and Elvira went to Syman where he had been born and raised. It was inevitable, given the terms of the cease-fire, that the peace would be a transient one, for there were many like Billy Cashin who could not sleep in their beds within the confines of such a pact.

In the civil war which ensued, the Bishop of Syman excommunicated all those who would not abide by the signed document. But they went ahead anyway and took control of large parts of the west, where the pro-cease-fire troops soon dared not go. So many postal deliveries were ambushed that the drivers drove their vans to the edge of the rebel territories and walked away, leaving the keys in the ignition and the doors unlocked. It was an arrangement which worked well until the pro-cease-fire troops loaded a mail-bag with explosives which they detonated with time-switches. This was how Billy Cashin met his death. It had been a very pleasant afternoon. The ambush had been a friendly one and the van driver had enjoyed the whiskey and sandwiches the rebels brought him. There had been a sort of picnic at the side of the road, during which the revellers had been blown to pieces by the exploding mail-bag. Elvira Poxon took what was left of her husband back to the parish church at

Syman where she was refused entry by Father Raphael Oberon, who said that if it was up to him he would accept the remains without question but that the Bishop had spoken and the rebels were excommunicated, so they could not be given funeral rites on church property. Elvira Poxon pleaded with the old priest. 'You were here when he was born,' she said. 'You washed away his original sin when you poured the water of the Sea of Galilee on his head and he cried in your arms. You were here when he first swallowed Christ. You made him a soldier for God and he swore to you that he would not drink alcohol until he was twenty-one and he kept his promise. He came here and whispered his most personal sins to you and you told him that God forgave him and he believed you. He confided in you as a man does in no one else, and now that he is dead you tell me that he cannot come in any more.' Father Raphael Oberon told her that his heart bled for her. He told her that he would eat the moon if that would make it possible for him to let them pass. But his hands were tied so tight his wrists bled, and so Billy Cashin was buried in unconsecrated ground without a priest.

Some weeks later, the Bishop of Syman came to consecrate the new roof of the church. When he entered the building, it was crowded with people who feared him. He walked up through them, blessing them as he went, until he reached the pulpit where he could begin his mammoth homily. It was a Halley's Comet of a sermon, returning to the same points again and again over long periods of time. The timbers in the new roof aged considerably during it. It fertilised the eggs of headaches and pregnant women were noticeably larger as they left. Christ fell a fourth time on the Stations of the Cross, as the Bishop spoke of the Godlessness of rebellion. As he did so, Elvira Poxon sat at the grave of Billy Cashin, knowing from the peace it brought her that he had gone to heaven despite the best efforts of the man in purple.

That was why Elvira Poxon did not mind when Erno Wellbeloved received acclaim for ideas which were hers, and why she now devoted her life to the trivial hobby of helping create westerns. Important things no longer mattered to her. They were dangerous and people got hurt around them. She confined herself to the banal and the useless because they were safe – as was Erno Wellbeloved. For all his ideas of being remembered, he was a banal person who did not possess the capacity to hurt her. I told her that I thought this was a terrible way for her to spend the rest of her life. She was intelligent and worthy of better things. She only said that maybe some day history would prick the conscience of God's men and they would undo the damage they had done when they excommunicated the rebels and sent Billy Cashin's body away from their door. Until that day, she said, other people would be guilty of far greater pettiness than she.

It was only when I could see Stockholm that I began to give serious thought to how I would first react when I met Rory Brophy. It was a long time since we had seen each other, so I decided that a big hug would not be out of place. When we did meet, though, it was probably embarrassment and unease that made the encounter so much less dramatic. He saw me first and called my name in a less than frantic way. He was pleased to see me, but it was not in the nature of our relationship to indulge in emotional scenes, so we contented ourselves with expressions of happiness at seeing each other and then he took me for a drink.

Rory drank in a fashion which showed him to be no novice. Max Sponge joined us in the evening and asked me if I knew anything about Swedish history. When I replied 'absolutely nothing', he laughed and said, 'Good, good, you're perfect for the job.' Rory Brophy was, in fact, genuinely happy to see me and he had a lot to tell me about his new home. He never mentioned his old one; it was a closed area in his mind, one where he had not even been able to kill himself properly. He was too happy for me to spoil it for him on the first day, so I concealed my real reason for coming. This was the most contented Rory Brophy I had ever seen. He had put on a little weight, though he still looked like a lamp-post. I let him do most of the talking as we left sobriety behind. As I listened I began to question whether I had done the right thing, whether I had any right to come and ask him to give up his new-found happiness and return with me to a place where he had been so miserable. All the time he kept saying to me, 'Tomorrow I have something to show you.' When we went home to his apartment it was dark and extremely cold. He still lived on the Rindo Gatan, but was now in a place above an accountant's office which was above two solicitors' offices. His apartment was decorated with pictures of Marilyn Monroe and Marlon Brando. He made me coffee, which warmed me delightfully, and we then collaborated in the lighting of a fire, during which he kept saying that he had something to show me the next day.

When I woke up in the morning I had a sore head

and my throat was so dry it hurt to swallow. The room was unrecognisable even though I knew I must have seen it the night before with the light on. I did not remember going to bed, but my clothes were neatly folded on the chair beside me. I almost felt disappointed with myself, for even in a state of drunkenness I had still remembered to fold them so they would not be creased in the morning. It was an automatic thing for me to do, an involuntary movement of my arms . . . And there they lay, like they belonged to a good soldier. I was on my own in the apartment. It was midday and there was a smell of old bacon in the kitchen which made my stomach feel ill. I needed a walk. Some fresh air would clear my head and fix me up. I took one of Rory's coats, which was too long for me but fashion was of no concern to me then. As I had no particular idea of where to go, I memorised the face on a clock-tower near the apartment which would be my compass, and set off in the direction of a widening in the road. There were many things about Rory's condition which impressed me and came to the surface of my mind as I walked.

What was most extraordinary for me was the gulf which had opened between our mental ages. I was seventy-eight days older than him, seventy-eight and a quarter to be exact. Both our arrivals had been momentous. The first sounds I must have heard were the Angelus bells. My father told me that I arrived on the peal of the third bell of the second threesome. He took this as a sign that I was destined to be a priest and referred to me in my first few months as his 'little Pope', until my grandmother objected to such blasphemy and insisted he was to stop. It was an insult to her that anybody should make such flippant use of the name of the highest office of Catholicism, let alone compare a babbling, shitting infant with the Holy Father himself – he who she adored with such fervour and whose picture hung on her bedroom wall like a missing sweetheart. Even though I was her grand-child she would not allow me to be compared to the Vicar of Christ. She died when I was less than two, so I have no memories of her. I am told by people in candid moments that she was completely devoid of any sense of humour. In my early days she repeatedly made it clear that I was an insignificant blob when compared to he whose picture hung on her wall, and on the few occasions when I have had to visit her grave, I have been tempted to fart, and only refrained out of respect for the dead.

Born at midday I was, midday on the peal of the sixth chime. Half-way through the day, half-way through the Angelus. Born in the middle to mediate, a broker by birth. Now I was taking the biggest chance of my life in accordance with the wishes of the planets which had brought me into being with the day lodged symmetrically on either side of me. I was a neutral being, my personality gelded so that I would be of no use other than for consoling others, listening to their problems and advising solutions – just as I had done so many times for Rory, whose mother had turned up at my birth to see for herself what was in store for her. She thought it such a moving thing that the Angelus rang during the event that she cried for me and my mother. She told me during the search for Rory that every day when Peebo the Sacristan rang the Angelus at midday, she would think of me for one minute and I once calculated that she had spent four days, three hours and eighteen minutes of her life thinking of

171

nothing else but me. She wished at the time of my birth that her own pregnancy would end with the mystique of the Angelus bells ringing in her ears. When her day came and the doctor told her that it could happen at any time, she watched the clock edge up to midday. She heard the bells peal . . . and then thought that maybe it would happen at six. In the early afternoon things began to occur and she knew that she would not hold out. Rory Brophy was delivered at eight minutes to five.

Seventy-eight and a quarter days older than him I was and that extra maturity had always been obvious up to the moment he jumped off the flyover. It seemed, however, that I had ceased to be older than him somewhere between the time his feet left the flyover and the moment he landed on the satsumas, for by that time he had become older than me. All the advice I had listened to about making sure not to miss school and be diligent about homework. All the extra hours I had spent being a conscientious student because there would come a day when I would be rewarded for my efforts and thank all those who had offered such sterling advice. All of that was rendered redundant the moment Rory Brophy tried to leap to his death and jumped into a magnificent new world where sensible people never went, but which glorified the art of living far more than did the accumulation of knowledge for the sake of modest gains. Walking down a road in a strange city I wondered if the bells had rung in the ears of the wrong baby. Perhaps my grandmother had been right. Perhaps as I lay and burbled up at her, she had seen something which made it obvious to her that I was not going to amount to anything special; that as my contemporaries grabbed the world by its heels and shook it upside-down so that every piece of excitement fell out on to the ground, I would stand by as a spectator. Was her lack of humour the result of clairvoyancy? Had she crystal balls for eyes which looked into the future and saw nothing for me but abundant insignificance?

This was the thing which worried me (and I use the word 'worried' after some consideration). It was not jealousy, at least I hoped not. No, I am certain. I was very happy for Rory Brophy. It was good to see him in such high spirits. His was a sad story which had had a happy ending, in so far as the present is the end. I did not wish we could switch places; that would have been unfair to him. I genuinely believed he deserved the happiness which had come his way. I knew that this kind of happiness is not in limited supply. It only needed proper cultivation, just like my grandfather's garlic. You had to plant the cloves to reap the harvest. I did feel reflected happiness from having spent the previous day with Rory, but there would come a time when I would have to leave and go back to where his aura would not reach me any more.

I came across a large square with car-park markings on the ground, but which had been taken over by a circus with a big top and several smaller tents placed around it. At one of these small tents, no more than ten-foot square, a woman sitting outside told me that I could have my fortune told, 'For better for worse, for young or for old, for five pence a head, your future foretold.' I went in and sat on one of a short row of seats with a curtain in front of me, behind which sat Olin the Clairvoyant, whose head was silhouetted against the curtain and whose face I never saw. He sat sideways to me and when the light went on behind him he began. He dropped his head back and drew in a long, slow breath which created a terrible wail in his throat. When he breathed out it stopped but began again with his next gasp. He told me that he saw death and I must be careful. I must leave at once and go far away. Someone would die and it could be me. All he could tell me was that I must go and go quickly. Then his light went out and I was again in darkness. I was annoyed at him and shouted that this was robbery. I had paid good money and had been told that I may die; he must tell me more, be more specific. There was no reply from behind the curtain, so I spoke again and this time he answered. 'No more information, Sir, I can tell you no more. Please, please go.'

I confess to being deeply disturbed by the revelation of Olin the Clairvoyant. This was perhaps because it came at a time when my comparative shortcomings were uppermost in my mind. But it was also because I had a habit of only believing such people on the occasions when they predicted death. This habit had its origin in happenings at the Belly Deli, which was a restaurant near where we lived. The Belly Deli was the *de facto* office of a man called Nacio Moloney, who was in his mid-forties and always dressed in a long, dark coat and woollen hat comprised of horizontal hoops in rastafarian colours. He was a man of genius when it came to telling things about people, or so he claimed. He referred to himself as the Janus of fortune-telling because he could see both past and future. The ambi-dextrous seer had wandered into the Belly Deli during a thunderstorm on 10 September with no money and smelling of life in the dustbins of Yivon. He made it clear to Georgie Kampfeart, the proprietor, that he had no money to pay for the coffee and sandwich he had just eaten, but was deeply sorry for Georgie and commiserated with him on the death of his father in a riding accident on 9 September, forty-one years previous. To say the least, Georgie was stunned that this man should know of his personal history in such detail. He was also embarrassed as he had forgotten that the previous day was the anniversary of his father's death. He wasn't sure whether to cry or box the insolent customer in the face for intruding into his personal grief in such a casual way.

When he had regained his senses, Georgie Kampfeart stormed down to the table to which Nacio Moloney had returned. He said to him, 'Now wait just a minute. Who the hell do you think you are, coming in here and saying such a thing?' Nacio Moloney asked him if he had made a mistake, but before Georgie Kampfeart could answer, Nacio said, 'No, it was definitely the ninth of September. I am right, amn't I?' The deli owner could only gasp at such impertinence. How dare this total stranger know the date of his father's death when he himself had forgotten it? But again Georgie was unable to speak before the uppity customer reminded him that his mother's anniversary was in three weeks' time; he even knew that she had died of pneumonia in the nursing-home of the Sisters of Charity eighteen years ago.

This was more than Georgie Kampfeart could take. He was not a violent man by nature, because he was quite small and was certain to lose any fight he might get into. But he was mad – no, he was very mad, his rage almost unprecedented. I say 'almost' because of the time he became so annoyed with his neighbour for repeatedly playing the same Caruso record for five days that Georgie fired a stone at the man's cat and killed it. This was followed by a day of such remorse that he became a vegetarian. But Georgie was that mad again. He lost control of himself, grabbed the stranger's woollen hat and ran behind the counter with it. There he buried it deep in a bowl of mushroom and onion coleslaw before returning it full to Nacio's head. But Georgie was immediately gripped by remorse again, and offered to clean Nacio's hat and not to call the police on him for eating the sandwich and drinking the coffee without paying. Nacio was immediately satisfied with the offer and assured the little restaurateur that there were no hard feelings. He said that Georgie's reactions were completely understandable under the circumstances, and the two men shook hands.

It was then that Nacio made an offer which Georgie was happy to accept. It was that he should entertain the Deli's customers with clairvoyancy in return for a hot meal every day. This became a very successful arrangement. News of a resident seer offering his services for nothing brought huge crowds to the Belly Deli. The numbers grew to such an extent that Georgie Kampfeart hired some builders to knock out a side wall and create seating for an extra twenty people.

Nacio Moloney sat in the same seat every day, two tables away from the door with his back to the wall and an impressionist water-colour of a field of convolvulus minors above his head. This was the work of Elizabeth Disraeli, who described herself as a structuralist-functionalist artist and usually lost business because of it. Beneath this example of her work, in the restaurant of one of her few patrons, Nacio Moloney spent his days with his nose buried in tea cups, where the tea leaves spoke to him and revealed elements in the past and future of whoever sat opposite him. The tea-leaves were, in fact, spurious props to his show. He could tell nothing from them and dismissed those who made such claims. But he did like tea, and simply instructed his customer to buy him some whenever he felt like it. He had other props, too. When he became hungry, he developed the knack of seeing visions in the shape of a lettuce leaf plucked from a salad sandwich. The alignment of the seeds in a slice of tomato also held secrets which he could unlock, as did the number of wheat-germs which fell from a slice of wholemeal bread. None of these were of any use to Nacio Moloney, except to ensure that his belly remained constantly full of Georgie Kampfeart's excellent cuisine.

The source of Nacio Moloney's knowledge was never discovered, but he did have a way of seeing death, both in the past and in the future. An example was his informing Fidelma Astaire of the death of her Uncle Seth in the hills near Celia while hunting sixteen years before. The Astaire family had never been able to find out what happened to him after he had gone to fight in the Colonial War. Although the word of a clairvoyant was insufficient for the legal men to use as proof of his death, the story came as a great relief to the family, who believed it entirely and rested assured that their relative was not wandering lost somewhere.

When he spoke of death, Nacio Moloney was indeed very good. It was when he tried to see other events that his problems began. He arrived for work one morning and informed Georgie Kampfeart that he had made the decision to diversify. He asked Georgie if he was familiar with the word 'entropy'. Georgie looked at him in the negative. Entropy was a word which referred to the tendency for things to disintegrate into disorder if there were not a constant input of new ideas. Fortune-telling was like that. His talent would fade if he did not push himself all the time. So he had decided to 'see' other aspects of people's lives besides those concerning death. He confessed that this was not a totally new departure for him. Once, while telling Sigmund Burger of the imminent death of his prize greyhound, he had seen glimpses of white. It was like a flash or a dart of pain which lasted for a split-second. He took it to refer to a wedding, but felt too unsure of his information to say anything. He had been partially correct. Less than a month after the death of his valuable dog from a broken neck sustained while chasing a rabbit, a bitch it had covered gave birth to a litter of six pups, five of which were replicas of their magnificent sire. The sixth was an albino. This was a long way from a wedding, but Nacio had correctly seen the colour white. All he needed was more practice.

The move was not to prove successful for Nacio Moloney. The colour white continued to appear to him and he told Margaret Muir that very soon she would be married. As there was no man in her life at the time and she was not the sort of girl to get herself into trouble, she took this as a sign that she was about to be swept off her feet in a whirlwind romance of the kind described in the women's magazines she loved to read. Margaret Muir had been a devotee of Nacio Moloney ever since he had accurately spoken of the circumstances of her brother's death in America. The colour white in his vision was the news she had been waiting for, and she believed him to the extent that she commissioned a wedding dress from Sandra Hopkirk, who said she was delighted with the news and wished the couple years of happiness. But Margaret Muir was to find to her cost and her sadness that Nacio Moloney was not a competent predictor of love. Three years later, the wedding dress still hung unused in her wardrobe, while she ate toffees and became fat, so that there would be a reason why men did not love her.

This was one of a number of events which persuaded Nacio Moloney that he should stick to death as a topic of clairvoyance. Six months after he had predicted Margaret Muir's windfall of love, she returned to him in a most distressed condition and asked him if he was playing some sort of game with her. He assured her he was not. He had been convinced at the time of their last meeting that great things were in store for her in the field of romance. 'I can never be sure to the point of one hundred per cent,' he said. 'There is always room for error, and especially where affairs of the heart are involved. Love is so much more difficult to predict than death,' he said. 'It is brittle, like the crumbs of the almond biscuit that fell on my plate that day and told me that a man with so much love for you was within days of revealing himself. I am desperately sorry if you feel let down, but such is the way with these things.' Margaret Muir was inconsolable. At the age of thirty-three she had still never been held in a warm embrace by a man. This was not for the want of trying. She was a terribly nice person who would not have given a second thought to her own comfort if sparing it would make others happy. She was genuine when she expressed concern and she smiled a lot as she spoke. There was a theory that her smile made men uncomfortable. The idea of going through life with someone who smiled that much was not a pleasant one. 'Men like sadness in a woman,' said Vincent Towel. 'They like it when a woman cries, it makes them feel less vulnerable. A woman who smiles all the time has only one emotion. She is like a room with only one wall painted.' Whatever the reason, Margaret Muir was sure she was facing life as a spinster, which was the last thing she wanted and the reason why the fall of the almond crumbs had been such a tonic to her sad heart. Nacio Moloney's incorrect reading of them made her hate many things. She could never again enjoy the navy and violet beauty of a convolvulus minor as they were the flowers beneath which such a terrible trick had been played on her heart. Almond biscuits never again passed her lips because their crumbs lied. She grew to have a particular hatred for the planets which ultimately controlled everything. When her best friend Sinead Helmet commented one August night on the beauty of the harvest moon, she replied that the moon was shit. Such was her grief when she returned to Nacio Moloney that day that she asked him whether, if he could not predict love for her, he would please predict her death. Feeling on safer ground and staring at the seeds of a green pepper, Nacio told her that as far as he could see death was a long way off for her. This news came as yet another disappointment, so Nacio reminded her that he could not be sure to the point of one hundred per cent.

This unhappy encounter with Margaret Muir came

THE PALUXY RIVER THEORY

at a bad time for Nacio Moloney. He was at the time
under threat of court action from Pierre Casey, who
had gone into severe debt building an extension to his
public house on the advice of the clairvoyant – Nacio
had told him that he was sure the army was about to
construct a new base nearby. The thought of thirsty
soldiers with lots of money was a delightful one to the
brain of a publican, who dreamt about his new clien-
tele so much that he became worried that dormant
homosexual tendencies lurking in his genetic structure might have been released by the prospect of
taking money from fit young men in uniforms. But the
army never came and Pierre Casey faced bankruptcy.

These malfunctions in Nacio's new areas of explo-
ration convinced him that he must stick to death as his
source of inspiration. His credibility was quickly re-
established. Then one day he arrived for work and at
half past ten in the morning took as his first client an
atheistic life-insurance salesman who lived in a permanent state of crisis. He bought Nacio a bowl of
muesli so that the currants could predict how long he
had left to live, but when Nacio looked into it, it was
not the death of his customer that he saw, but his own.
He saw that he would die in a violent manner that
very afternoon. He left soon after, looking as pale as a
sheet as he said goodbye to Georgie Kampfeart. At
two in the afternoon, he returned to the crowded
restaurant, sat down beneath the flowers, pulled a
gun from his pocket and held it to his head. 'Look,
everybody,' shouted Nacio, 'look, see, Nacio Moloney is
the best clairvoyant of death alive.' Women began to
scream and people dived under the tables. Nacio pulled
the trigger and turned the convolvulus minors red.

The story of Nacio Moloney was the reason why I only had time for clairvoyants when they predicted death. It seemed to me that in this they were at least reliable so I left the tent of Olin the Clairvoyant in a state of some shock. I must have been pale and in a daze because I do not remember the walk back to Rory's apartment. I felt as if I were sleep-walking in an unfamiliar place. I knew where to go even though I had never travelled that way before. If the death Olin had predicted were mine, then it could easily have happened then as I wandered aimlessly through the busy streets. When I got back to Rory's apartment, I made myself some tea. It was the only thing I could think of which could offer me some solace at that time. Only with a cup gripped between my hands could I begin to tell myself that this was a nonsense. Olin would have said that to any person who went in there, and it was pure chance that the person happened to be me. This was all ridiculous, a paranoid consequence of my delicate condition following the consumption of so much alcohol the previous day, exacerbated by my genuine worry about the direction my life was taking in comparison to my contemporary.

When Rory Brophy returned he was in an excited mood and he asked me if I had slept well, eaten breakfast and gone into the city. He apologised for leaving me alone that morning, but he had had business to attend to. A party of South Koreans had arrived earlier than expected. They were terrible footballers, but had lots of money and tipped very well. In contrast to his buoyant mood, I was a picture of anxiety and he eventually calmed down enough to notice. He asked me what the problem was. Was I homesick? If so, it was entirely understandable; but I would have such a good time in Stockholm that I would never wish to go home again. He imagined that it must have been harder for me to leave than for him. He had hated it so much that he had jumped from the flyover, but I had always seemed to be happy there. He told me that when we were growing up he had always envied me. I seemed to know what to do all the time. I was never afraid and people always respected me. When he went to bed at night after a long day as the butt of so many jokes, he would play a game in which he pretended to be me. He remembered a day when his grandmother asked him, for some inexplic- able reason, which family he would most like to be in and he had no hesitation in saying mine. So it was perfectly understandable that I should be a little upset about having left all that behind and come into a strange world on the strength of his letter. I had to stop him talking and insist that my mood had nothing to do with homesickness. It was because of my encounter with the clairvoyant who had seen death. I was afraid for both of us because, like me, he too knew of the events at the Belly Deli and of the accuracy of these people when they spoke of death.

For the first time since we had known each other, Rory Brophy was able to console me. He reassured me that the character who had upset me was a fake who came every year with the circus. He was dying of emphysema and the only way he could make a living was to lay back his head and inhale, pretending that the noises which came up from his lungs were the cries of corpses past or future. 'I have been there myself,' Rory told me. 'Every year he says the same things. People go to him out of charity more than anything else. He hasn't long left and I think the only death he sees is his own.' Such was the confidence of this revitalised Rory Brophy that I did feel better having spoken to him. How much things had changed, and how I loved him for what he had achieved! 'I have something to show you today,' he said, 'but first we will eat. Talking to foreigners makes me hungry.' We prepared a meal and he refused to answer any of my questions about what I was going to be shown. 'Think of it as your dessert,' he said.

After we had eaten, we walked to a bus-stop near his apartment and waited ten minutes for the right bus to arrive. Rory paid the fares – I had still not put my hand in my pocket since my arrival in Stockholm. I thought that this might be the time to tell him the real reason why I had come, that I had no intention of staying, and that as he had accepted my advice in the past, he should do so again and come back with me. At least he should let his family know that he was alive. If he told them that he was getting on so well, I was sure they would be delighted and leave him be. His mother was a good woman who did not deserve to be treated this way. I wanted to tell him about her mental state, about how she had deteriorated, in the years since his disappearance, from being a vibrant woman who mobilised people so that the 'Justice bastards' would not be able to built a monstrosity at the end of the road and stop the sun shining in my grandfather's garden at midday. I wanted to tell him the tragedy of this great woman who had almost led the stoning of the beautiful dissident and sacrificed her lifetime collection of china artefacts so that it would be clear to all that political opportunism had no place in her house. What a sight it was to see such a person reduced to wandering through the ruins of hairdressing salons, calling out the name of her child and begging him to come home because she loved him so much. I wanted to tell him that this was not only a tragedy, but it was wrong and it had to stop.

And there was his father, who had that most thankless of jobs, bus conductor. It would be enough to drive anyone insane, even if they had the most wonderful family. Even life in the happiest home would not compensate a man for earning a living collecting fares on overcrowded buses in the dead heat, listening to the abuse of passengers who treated him like dirt. On top of all that, his father had been expected to do the most difficult thing ever asked of men, namely, to hide sorrow when tidal waves of tears are smashing and breaking against the backs of their eyes. I wanted to ask Rory Brophy how this could be justified. How could any happiness be built on such a foundation and at such a price? I wanted to ask him all those things but, given the euphoric state I found him in, to bring them up would be to usher in a very bad period for him. As the bus took us to wherever we were going, I became aware again of the trouble I had gotten into. Everything was unclear, completely unclear.

We were on the bus for thirty minutes. Rory passed the time by pointing out the sights to me: museums and galleries, famous shops, the best restaurants and bars, picture houses, the dangerous areas where I shouldn't go alone, if at all. I have always had a bad sense of direction and was sure that none of this would mean anything to me afterwards – I had just about grasped the layout of my own city after nearly twenty years. When we got off, we were in a quieter area than the one we had started from. The streets were tree-lined, with four-storey buildings on either side and small gardens at the front. There were very few people about, just the odd one or two walking their dogs and carrying shopping. He showed me to number 18 and took a key from his pocket. We went up to the second floor where he unlocked a door at the top of the stairs. Inside there was a large room which was bright and empty of furniture and smelt of paint. Rory walked to the middle of the room and laughed. He asked me what I thought of his new home. The whole floor was his: five rooms, including a bathroom and kitchen. I replied that I was impressed, and I was. The view from the window was . . . peaceful, lots of trees. He told me that he had finished painting and would move in in a few days.

His second surprise of the day was that I could have his old apartment in the Rindo Gatan. 'Just imagine,' he said, 'a place of your own. How long have you dreamt of such a thing? The freedom, not having to think about other people who share the same place. Do what you want. Eat when you want. Throw things where you want. This is it, boy, you and me. We're the ones who made it. We're the ones that escaped. None of those smart-arsed bastards who thought they knew everything. None of those shit-heads who left the imprint of their boots on my backside. None of those cocky sons of bitches who thought they had a divine right to be superior. What are they doing now? I'll tell you. They're filling out application forms for jobs in the tyre factory or one of those offices down in the city, that's what they're doing. That's where their cockiness got them, and no further. But you and me, we're a team, we always have been. I've never forgotten you for not taking part when they picked on me. I will always remember you for asking them to stop and leave me alone. You probably thought I never noticed. You probably thought I regarded you as one of them. But no, I never did, you were never like them. You were always different, better than them, much better. I noticed you never hit me; you were the only one. A person notices these things. You always remember the face of the one that beats you, and yours was never one of them. That's why you were the only one I would write to when Max Sponge asked me if I knew anyone who would take the job. I knew I could trust you. I knew you wouldn't tell – you haven't, have you? You and me together. We're a team, we always have been. I'm so glad you're here. You've made things even more perfect.'

Rory made tea. He too was a devotee of its ability to suit every emotion. When he had brought his ladder and paint to decorate his new home, he had also brought a kettle, for no such work was thinkable without regular intakes of the magic of the cup that cheers. We sat on the window-ledge with a large, empty white room in front of us. Rory's speech had left me numb. I was flattered that he should think of me in such a way and could see how much it meant to him that I was here. But I could also see how precious his new life was to him. I knew I had to speak my mind before the problem was compounded. I felt sure that he could have the best of both worlds. He could let the people at home know that he was alive and well and still live as he did. With the courage of a mug of tea in my hand, I gasped the air and asked him if he would make some contact with home and let them know he was all right.

His reaction surprised me. I thought he might get angry but he didn't. He remained calm and shook his head. 'It is impossible,' he said. What he had here was based on a frame of mind. His confidence was new to him. He asked me if I had ever seen him so confident and happy. I had to answer 'No' and he told me that this proved his point. Confidence was in the mind. His had come because he had made a clean break, a fresh start. It was as clean a break as when the doctor had severed his umbilical cord. The old Rory Brophy no longer existed. He had vanished from the face of the Earth. He had tried to kill himself by jumping off a flyover. Anyone who went as far as that was entitled to do whatever they wanted to afterwards. He had almost paid the ultimate price, so he owed nothing to anyone. He was a free man and the world should expect no dues from him, just as the hangman should expect no thank you from the condemned because the trapdoor jammed. His past was over and any contact with it would open the floodgates of suffering again. Even thinking or talking about it upset him. 'Besides,' he said, 'the worst is over for everyone. It certainly is for me, and for them too. It's been years, they'll all be over it now. My mother will be back making rabbit-stew and organising people to stop this or start that. My father will be whistling his way through another day's work. My sister never liked me anyway because all I ever did was fart on her head in the mornings. My father will be retiring in a few years. He'll be a pen-sioner. They always said that when he retired they would buy a house in the country. That will be great for them. I'm sure there are plenty of things that need to be done in the country, so my mother will be kept busy. There will be plenty of long roads for my father to go for walks along. They'll love it, it's what they've always wanted.'

It was clear that Rory Brophy was completely ignorant of the realities of what he had left behind. I told him that he was totally wrong if he believed that he was forgotten and that people didn't care about what had happened to him. I had to tell him the reason why I had come. It was not to join him in his new life. I was grateful that I was the one he had chosen to write to. I was humbled by his trust, and had not said a word to anyone. It was true that we were a team, that we had stuck together, but how could we be partners in such a plot? How could we inflict such sorrow on people who didn't deserve it? It was no revenge on the idiots who had plagued him. They didn't give a damn that he was missing, in fact they probably sniggered amongst themselves that they always knew Rory Brophy was so stupid that one day he would get himself so lost he would never be found again. It was no kick in their teeth, unless they knew that not only was he alive, but also thriving and happy. But they were unimportant anyway, he shouldn't concern himself with them. What about his mother? I told him that she was far from getting over his disappearance. I told him she was going mad with loneliness, being found wandering in disused shops calling his name. His father, too – he had turned every busman in the city into an amateur detective. How could he think that they would forget him? So that was why I had come. If I was so against what he had done, how could I do the same myself? I had come to try to persuade him to return with me, or at least to let me tell people what had happened.

He was furious with me. He was disappointed with me. I had betrayed his trust. I did not understand him. I was not as clever as he thought. There was no way that he would do what I asked. Going home was absolutely out of the question, as was letting people know. He held me to the promise I had made when I read the opening lines of his letter. Then he said that he had one more thing to show me. He grabbed his coat and stormed out of the room shouting at me to follow him. I asked him where we were going. 'Home,' he yelled from the bottom of the stairs. We went back into the street and stood for another bus. We didn't speak. Rory was still very angry and he couldn't stand still. He fidgeted and shuffled around until the bus came. We went back the way we had come but this time there was no guided tour. We remained silent. I was miserable. This was all getting too much. I should have burnt his letter and minded my own business, or brought it straight to his mother and none of this would ever have happened. I cursed the stars that had brought me into the world at mid-day on the sixth peal of the Angelus. I was fed up with being in the middle. It was no fun. People took advantage of you and thought that you had no feelings of your own. I was no saint and this was not my vocation.

When we got back to the apartment that was supposed to be mine, Rory had cooled down and spoke with more sadness than anger. He had many plans. There were lots of places he wanted to take me, not just in the city but out in the country, up in the mountains. Beautiful places where he had spent many weekends with Max Sponge and the Furtwangler Kickers. They jokingly referred to these places as their 'training camps', but all they ever did there was drink and sing. They had had such good times, and Rory had wanted me to be part of it. But that was not going to happen now. He said that he presumed I would go straight back. He was sad that none of his plans would come to fruition – especially after he had told everyone about me, about how much more intelligent I was than him, how I would bring some style to the operation. They had all expressed great interest in meeting me because the Furtwangler Kickers were nothing if not some of the nicest men on earth. There was something about men who had been made redundant in middle age, when it was difficult for them to get another job – there was a real earthiness about them. They knew they were lucky to have an entrepreneur like Max Sponge to pass some money to them during difficult times and so a wonderful spirit ran through the whole outfit. I would be the worse for not being part of it . . . but that was my decision.

It was a measure of Rory's emotional state that when we reached his apartment he made more tea while we spoke. Then he added vodka to it while we drank. We sat in his living room on the wooden bench with the striped cushions. Large amounts of time we spent in silence. They were unusually uneasy periods because, as children, we had spent long periods together in total silence without them ever being tense. Silence had been as much a part of our friendship as conversation. We understood it not to be a sign of boredom or aloofness. But this time there was a feeling that I had not experienced with him before. Things had changed, this was a new time for us both.

We had drunk several cups of tea and vodka when I heard a key turn in the lock. Rory was up and out of his chair before the key completed its rotation. By the time the door was opened, he was out in the hall. Max Sponge, I thought to myself. This had originally been his apartment so he probably still had a key. I heard Rory say hello and then there were footsteps in the kitchen and the door was closed behind them. This was the lowest point for me yet. They were in there and Rory was explaining to Max about the treachery behind my journey. He was apologising for me, telling Max that the friend he had spoken so highly of was nothing but a charlatan who had come like a Trojan horse with poison concealed in his belly. Their plans for expansion would have to wait; I was a set-back, a big disappointment, but I would be gone in the morn-ing and they could start a new search for someone with guts who recognised a good opportunity when they saw it. I needed more tea but they were in the kitchen, so my supply was cut off. What a mess this was, what an unholy mess. I finished what was in my cup and then began to drink Rory's, which was bitter because he took no sugar. Then I heard the kitchen door open. They had decided what to do with me. At that moment I was close to tears for us all. I was aware that they were standing behind me, but my head would not unlock to turn around. Rory called my name and the only way I could manage to look at him was by twisting my whole torso around and taking my head with it.

There stood Rory Brophy, my erstwhile friend who had offered me a place in the sun because the victim always remembers the face of the ones who hit him and I had not been one. Standing beside him: not Max

Sponge nor any of the Furtwangler Kickers; not even a male, but a young woman. She was tall and quite thin, but not to the ridiculous extent that Rory was. Thin, that is, in the arms and legs and neck, but not in the stomach. She was heavily pregnant and looked so big that I guessed she should be in bed with a midwife standing by with towels and a basin of hot water. She had a smile on her face which was not at all menacing, and her presence relaxed me. Rory was smiling also, and so did I. The three of us stood there smiling at each other for what seemed like an age before Rory put his arm around her shoulder and told me that this was Abby, who was pregnant with their child and they would be married soon.

I can't remember what I did then. It was probably stupid because I was so overcome with surprise. I had never imagined Rory Brophy as a person with a sexual drive, the two just didn't seem to mix, but here he was standing beside his wife-to-be with their baby ready to be born. The first thing I can remember was being so terribly happy for him and then for them. I had always liked it when babies were born. It seemed to have a cleansing effect on people. It refilled them, replenished them. I went over to Rory and threw my arms around him and he hugged me and we laughed and cried. I shook hands with Abby and was generally clumsy, but then gave her a hug and told them I was delighted for them. 'I'll make tea,' I said, 'I'll make a huge pot.'

We drank my brew, mixing it with vodka. Because I did not know Abby, I began by addressing all my questions to Rory, but she was not shy and made me feel like one of her old friends. She had that gift of making you like her instantly. Her English was quite good and she told me the stories that Rory had told her about me. He had flattered me completely. He must have made them up because I had no recollection of the events she recounted. What I was most interested to know was when the baby was due to be born. 'A few weeks,' she said, after which they would move into their new apartment. They would be married next week, with Max Sponge as best man, and there was still an invitation for me if I wanted to come. I said I couldn't refuse but had very little money. This was not a problem. I could be taken care of and . . . Perhaps I might even give some renewed thought to the original plan? 'Just think of what things would be like,' implored Rory, 'what times we could have, good times. We will have money and money means laughs. We can go to the country for weekends with the baby – you always loved babies. I want you to be godfather. How could you say no to such a life? You will find nothing like it at home, just a job in the tyre factory or one of the offices in the city. Here you can live like the king of opportunity with your godchild growing up near you.' I told him I would think about it. It is true that the birth of children seems to change things.

On the few occasions that Abby left the room that evening, I plagued Rory with questions. Why had he kept this a secret from me? Where had they met? How long had he known her? He was relaxed, like a king after a banquet, his face beaming with contentment. 'All in good time,' he told me. Abby would be going home at the weekend and we would go into the city and spend the day drinking, during which he would tell me everything. There was a lot to tell and it would take time.

The night went quickly and when I went to bed, I

felt dizzy from the vodka, but I was proud at the prospect of being a godfather. Lying in bed in the room of the apartment that had been planned in the scheme of things to be mine, I could see the vision that Rory Brophy had pieced together. He was a man (he certainly was now) who had never found it easy to make friends. He was naturally suspicious of them because of the way he had been treated. He could only protect himself from a lonely life by bringing those friends he had closer to him. It was clever really. I tried to imagine how he must have been feeling at that moment, lying in the other room with the woman who would soon be his wife and his child growing inside her. This was indeed a triumph for him. I could see why it was impossible for him to go home. It must have been of paramount importance to him that he protect Abby and his new child from the life he had led. Happiness was such a fragile thing for him. It had not come easily, but only on the other side of a failed attempt at suicide. Who was I to ask him to bring his young wife and child back, even for a brief time, to that place where he had been so unhappy? I saluted him as one of the bravest and most considerate men I knew.

6 *A Fly at the Window*

I did not see much of Abby between that night and the weekend. She worked in a bookshop in the Vasa Gatan which opened early in the morning and closed at nine o'clock at night. On one of the days I had not much else to do, I went in to see the shop and wander around it. I spent an hour there. Abby was busy the whole time. I was afraid she was working too hard in her condition, but they needed the money.

On Saturday morning, Rory came into my room and told me that this was the day he would tell me all he had to about how he met Abby. He confessed that his account of meeting Max Sponge on his second day in Stockholm had not been quite accurate. What had occurred had occurred all right, but after two weeks and not two days. What happened in those two weeks was what he had to tell me now. We ate a good breakfast as he told me I would need it, then we left for a part of the city which I recalled he had warned me against visiting alone. I reminded him of this and he said that I was not alone and that, in any case, it was Saturday morning. No one ever got attacked on Saturday morning. It was an unwritten code amongst the muggers, perhaps because they were too tired after

197

Friday night, their busiest time of the week, but at six o'clock on Saturday morning all mugging stopped and the old people felt it was safe to come out. It was in one of these streets that he had received his first beating by a foreigner, and it had happened, uniquely, on a Saturday morning. 'There are certain reasons why I will never forget what time it happened at,' he said.

He had been in the city only three days when he woke up in an alcove at the front of a large, ornate building, the premises of a bank. There was a wonderfully florid iron balustrade running across the alcove about two feet off the ground. It had the heads of demons wrought on it, and spikes sticking out in all directions. The bar was designed to keep tramps from climbing into the alcove and sleeping there at night. It was funny how the meanness of the bank's owners had inspired such art. However, the physique of Rory Brophy allowed him to slip beneath the spikes, where he found the small alcove to be quite comfortable. It was clean, too, because no one had ever got in there before. It sheltered him from the breeze which had made his teeth chatter so much that one of them had broken and he had developed a cramp in his jaw. When he sat down against the wall of the alcove and pulled his knees up to rest his head on, he was very content. 'This will be a comfortable night,' he thought. It would have been had he not been continually pestered by the tramps. He would doze off to sleep only to be wakened by a prod in the head. A tramp would be standing outside the bar with a stick in his hand, insisting that Rory tell him how to get in there. Every hour he was woken by tramps, whose received wisdom it was that the only way to get behind the bar was to crawl beneath it as a child and grow up in there. They were sure that Rory had not done this. One of them even urinated on him to express their communal envy at him for solving the puzzle. It was not until he stood up that they could observe his physique, which gave away the secret of his successful entry.

The sight of Rory Brophy inspired a new mood amongst the tramps. They began to spurn the hot soup and bread that the charities brought to them at night. Many of them became anorexic, refusing to eat in case they put on weight. They stopped rooting through the bins at the back doors of restaurants. Some of them took to exercising regularly, sprinting up and down the lanes wearing several coats so that they would sweat and lose weight. All of this so they would be able to crawl beneath the spikes and sleep in the alcove at night. This continued until one of them made a premature effort to enter the alcove. But it turned out he had an exaggerated opinion of his thinness. He lay on his back and began to slide beneath the bar. He exhaled so much his face turned puce and reflected off the wall. But it wasn't enough, he needed more sprints up the lanes. He pushed and heaved so that the points dug into his ribs. Then, during a final effort to make it to the far side, a spike pierced his heart and he died like a vampire. Art kills sometimes. The bank's owners removed the bar and bricked up the alcove.

This happened long after Rory's days as a tramp. On the morning he had first inspired the craze for slimming, having been urinated upon, he left the alcove in a wet and smelly condition. He had no idea where he was going, so he followed the streets where the sun shone so he could dry himself. This walk took him down into the area where you shouldn't go alone. He passed the fish shop of Walter Rattigan, who was closing up for the day because he was sold out. This was a famous shop with very regular customers who came in the early hours to buy stock when it was fresh. By nine-thirty every Saturday morning, he was sold out and would close up for the day. Rory Brophy passed him as he locked the front door and got into his car.

The sound of Walter Rattigan's car was still to be heard when Rory was confronted by an extremely rough-looking man who was as wide as he was tall. He was six-feet square and demanded Rory's money. Rory tried to explain to him that he was penniless and had just been urinated on, but the assailant took no notice of him and proceeded to search his pockets. 'There was no one around to help me,' said Rory. 'Walter Rattigan's car was only a distant hum, so I just had to stand there and offer no resistance while he went through my trousers and coat.' The square man was extremely annoyed when he could find nothing and began to thump and kick Rory all over. Rory shouted for help, but no one heard him. When the man had beaten him up enough he walked off grumbling.

Rory stumbled into a café where he shouted to a waiter to phone the police because he had just been mugged. 'Don't be ridiculous,' said the waiter, 'it's only half past nine. No one gets beaten up before eleven on a Saturday. Now get out of here, you smell of piss.' The same thing happened to him when he found a policeman to report the crime. The officer of the law told him to go away or he'd arrest him for smelling so badly in a public area. It wasn't even ten o'clock and everybody knew that no one got attacked before eleven. This was all a bit upsetting for Rory at the time; but at a later stage, when he looked back and tried to make sense of it, he regarded it as an honour. He had made criminal history. He would have been in the record books, had anyone believed him. When he told the story a year later to the Furtwangler Kickers, they all laughed and called him a spoof – everybody knew it was safe before eleven.

In the aftermath of his encounter with the square man, Rory perceived crime in a different light. His situation was not so good after all. He was in a foreign country with no money, so the ingenuity of his own deceitfulness was his only immediate source of sustenance. His initial introduction to the life of a petty criminal had happened by accident, when he sat at a table with the remains of someone's coffee in front of him. It was a Sunday and the place was full of people who had come into the city to walk in the parks and throw bread to the ducks. A man put his coat and a leather bag on a seat beside Rory and said something which Rory presumed to be: 'Excuse me, but would you mind watching my bag and coat while I go to the counter?' Rory nodded and watched the man walk away to buy some cakes and tea. This was a curious thing that Rory had noticed. Not only were tourists trusted, but people also had a strange confidence in the integrity of those who sat at café tables. This man, however, had picked the wrong table. As he hovered his head above the pastry selection, peering down at them as if selecting one to wear on his head, foreign hands were roaming through his coat pockets: past his handkerchief and an old bus ticket and around the side of his door keys, where they found coins and bank notes to the value of a good hot meal. The man returned and thanked Rory for taking such care of his belongings. Rory nodded again, and left before the man finished his slice of cake.

Other luckless customers in restaurants went to the toilet during their meals only to return to find the remainder of their food gone. An old woman who arrived from the counter with her slice of cake quartered like a tennis court and who told Rory she was Belgian, asked him if he would mind watching her food while she went to the toilet to empty her colostomy bag. When she came back she found Rory in a panic. He was standing at the table with his mouth wide open, pointing to the door and then to the plate, where the tennis court lay with a large bite taken out of it so one of the service lines was completely missing. 'He went that way,' gasped Rory. 'My dear Belgian friend, I'm afraid it happened so fast I was taken by surprise, but a tramp has taken a bite out of your cake and run off that way.'

In the early hours of a Thursday morning, Rory Brophy woke up lying behind a skip full of construction sand and felt that this was the day that he was going to fall in love. 'I know for definite that it was a Thursday,' he said, 'because all the great things that have ever happened to me have happened on a Thursday. I was born on a Wednesday, and ever since that event in my life I have considered Wednesday to be my unlucky day. It was on a Wednesday that my Uncle Timothy died, when I was ten. In my younger years, before bad thoughts entered my mental vocabulary, I always thought that boys looked like their uncles and girls like their aunts. Because Uncle

Timothy looked so like me, I figured that physical characteristics were passed from uncle to nephew and auntie to niece. When Victor Jump told me that he had only one uncle who did not look the slightest bit like him, I told him this was impossible. How could he look like he did, then? 'Because my father looks like this,' Victor said. 'Then your father must be your uncle,' Rory said, so Victor Jump proceeded to hit him in the face for insulting his father. 'That was the first time anyone bar my parents hit me,' said Rory. 'It was on a Wednesday.' It was around the time that he reached twelve years of age that less-innocent reasons for the physical similarity between himself and his uncle occurred to Rory. The idea that his mother might have slept with her brother was repugnant to him, and his uncle began to notice that his erstwhile favourite nephew no longer wished to speak to him when they met. When he eventually asked Rory why they no longer joked like they used to, his nephew explained the thoughts which had been occupying him and had prevented him for laughing for ninety days. It was then that his uncle gave Rory his first lecture in genetics. By the time he was finished, the boy was happier than he had been for a long time. This happened on a Thursday. It was in the company of his uncle that he was happiest, and it was on a Wednesday afternoon that his mother came into the garden to tell him that his Uncle Timothy was dead.

Perhaps only on a handful of occasions in his life had Rory Brophy appeared to have greater talent than those around him. These flashes of his normally absent brilliance had all occurred on a Thursday. There was a 'Thursday of Mathematics', when numbers came to him in the correct sequence enabling him to solve an unsolvable equation in an exercise given by the mathematics teacher Hugo Card. He was a bachelor who had no interest in women. 'I am in love with numbers,' he said. 'You can trust numbers. They never lie to you. If I ever marry, it will be to the number eight because it is the number with the best figure.' Hugo Card had given his class an equation to solve but as he wrote it on the blackboard his thoughts were of number 8, and he wrote it down where he should have put a 6. Putting an 8 where there should have been a 6 rendered the equation unsolvable, but only to those who thought like a mathematician. The cleverest brains in the class spent hours that evening attempting to crack the problem, only to give up when their eyes could no longer stick the sight of it. In the classroom the following day, Hugo Card admitted his mistake. He apologised for the hours of frustration he had caused his pupils, many of whom sat sleeping with exhaustion. The teacher was privately becoming very concerned about his fixation with the number 8, which was taking over his life. He could not close a door once, he had to close it 8 times. It took him half an hour to dress in the morning because every piece of clothing had to be put on 8 times (he also got out of bed 8 times). If he had been a history teacher, this would not have been so difficult a problem (although he might have taken some liberties with the dates of important events), but as a mathematics teacher the fixation was now affecting his work. The incident with the unsolvable equation was just another manifestation of this. He was trying to conceal his worry from his class when Rory Brophy raised his hand and announced that between seven thirty and seven forty-five the previous night, he had solved the equation.

'But that is impossible,' said Hugo Card. 'It cannot be done where there is an eight where a six should be.' 'Then let me show you,' said Rory. He was handed the chalk and proceeded to make numbers lie. Hugo Card stood mesmerised as the steps unfolded, until Rory Brophy had done the mathematically impossible. He then declared his student either a genius or a liar, but he could not find anything wrong with the work in front of him. 'This is unbelievable, Rory . . . I can only award you the highest marks – eight out of eight.' The day he received this accolade was certainly the peak of academic achievement in Rory's education. But it was not to be repeated. Even the solution did not last, for when Hugo Card attempted to repeat it the following day in a letter to a mathematics journal, he could not make it come right. It was an equation which worked for just one day, a Thursday.

There were to be other days when the world looked favourably on Rory Brophy, days when he acquired the mastery of disciplines in an inexplicable way, like the 'Thursday of Music' when his boy-soprano voice, exercised on the toilet, germinated the cactus seeds his mother had planted in sand and left on the cistern behind the lavatory. She was told to give them plenty of time and she did, but they refused to obey the instructions of nature until the day that Rory Brophy sat with his back to them and sung 'When Twilight Comes I'm Thinking Of You' in such a beautiful fashion that the seeds believed it was the sun calling them, and up they came.

As well as having a brain which had once controlled numbers and a voice which had once controlled nature, Rory also had legs which had once carried him close to the speed of sound, or so it seemed. This happened after he was stopped outside the shop of Bernard Mason with a large bottle of lemonade in his hands. It was a swelteringly hot day and standing in front of him was Maurice Man, who was nothing short of a villain. He was not just a villain, but a very successful one at that, because he could run quicker than almost anyone so his victims rarely escaped. 'He could have been an Olympic runner,' his father told the judge at one of Maurice Man's trials, 'but he chose crime instead. Speed pays in sport and crime, I suppose.' When he was confronted by his attacker, Rory was surprised because he had a feeling in his waters that this was one of his good days. He refused to hand over the bottle. Maurice Man was not used to such impertinence. While he contemplated what to do next (his brain did not share his legs' capacity for speed), an extraordinary thing happened to the speedy criminal: Rory Brophy hit out and struck him just below the cheek-bone. It was hard to tell who got the bigger shock, but of all the limbs that were present, Rory Brophy's legs were the quickest to react. He took off up the road with the bottle of lemonade under his arm and, despite his best efforts, Maurice Man could not catch him. This was Rory Brophy's 'Thursday of Speed', the day he moved the fastest ever without mechanical assistance, and left crime trailing behind him.

These were the high points in Rory Brophy's life, the poles on which his tent was hung. Standing behind the skip of construction sand that morning, he could sense that the planets had aligned themselves overnight and were looking favourably on him again. He had had his moments in all of the great areas of human endeavour – science, art, sport – and now he felt that this was the day on which he would surpass himself in that other great field: love. When he climbed to his feet he could feel in his waters again that this was a day God had set aside for him. 'You may find this difficult to believe,' he said to me, 'that a man who has spent the night sleeping rough and wakes up with an empty stomach and no money, could even consider love. But the feeling was so strong, and it was a Thursday. I said this to the man who was lying beside me. I woke him up to tell him that this was my day and that within twenty-four hours I would meet the woman who would love me.'

At half past eleven he was mildly beaten up, but he didn't mind because he was so happy. Rory laughed as it took place and, as his attacker ran off, he lay on the ground and wished him a good day. He spent the morning wandering around the city centre, waiting for the incident which would bring him into contact with this mystery woman. Consumed with this feeling, he stepped in front of a car driven by a woman, who stuck her head out of the window to yell abuse at him. 'I am sorry, my darling,' he said to her and held his arms out towards her as if to say 'Here I am'. But she drove off.

In the open markets a woman selling carrots smiled at him in a manner which confused him as to what her intentions might be. He was hoping that she was not the woman who had been set aside for him. For Rory Brophy was a believer in grand designs. He followed instinct and not logic. He believed that love occurred at the nexus of time and destiny. From the moment of his birth, shortly before five o'clock on a Wednesday afternoon, he had felt like a passenger on a roller-coaster. He could not create love for himself if it was not meant for him, but this morning he had been gripped by an unmistakable feeling that all the years he had spent agonising about whether his life would end without having experienced the emotion that starts wars and inspires art (Rory was sure that all art was an expression of a desire to be loved), all that worry had been unnecessary. But could it possibly be that the bearer of this love was a woman who sold carrots and had a smile which confused? She was not pretty by any means, but his instincts told him that he must talk to her. The idea that he should ignore any instinct on such a crucial day was unthinkable. He thought to himself that if he did not speak to this woman and she was his pre-ordained lover, then he would never have another chance (love was only possible once). If she was the woman set aside by destiny, then they would get on famously, so he went over to her and told her that he had no money to buy any of her carrots but that he was very happy today because he was going to fall in love by midnight.

Unlike many of the hawkers, who would have sent him on his way for speaking such nonsense, the woman with the carrots answered him by saying that she hoped midnight would never come for him because there was no better feeling than that of imminent romance. This response alerted Rory to the possibility that he might indeed be standing in front of the woman of his destiny. 'How can imminent romance be better than love itself?' he said to her. 'I hope midnight comes soon because by this time tomorrow I will be wrapped in the warm blanket of the affections of a woman.' She told him that she thought love was like the bubbles a child blows from soapy water: they would never catch them again, but the fun was in trying. He told her that she was a melancholy woman and asked her if she had ever been in love. She replied that she had not, but that there had been many times when she had felt the way he did today. Many were the mornings she had woken up in the aftermath of a dream and felt that this was the day she would make great use of her heart, the day when bells would ring in her ears and an angel would come up behind her and discharge an arrow in her name. She would smile at men over her mound of carrots, which hid some of the inadequacies of her body and made a good vantage point from which to look at those who came to buy her wares. On those days when her expectations were greatest, the most handsome men took a liking to her carrots. Handsome and rich they would be, paying for what they bought with a note plucked from a thick wad. She would remind them that they must be careful carrying such sums of money in the markets (because a man likes a woman who is careful with money). They would thank her for her advice and she would smile at them and then they would leave. In the evenings she would return home empty of carrots and love, saying that instinct was rubbish. It was just a tease and not to be trusted.

Rory Brophy interrupted her to tell her that he was sure he knew the reason why she had been disappointed so many times. Instinct was not rubbish; instinct was truth, uncontaminated by concerns about wealth or status. It was innocent. 'It is not your instinct which has let you down, it is your smile,' he said to her. 'Your smile confuses people; it confused me. Today I am going to fall in love and I want everyone to know it. I don't know if you are the one I am going to fall in love with, but you must have been aware when you first saw me today that I was in a romantic state of mind. A smile is a periscope to the mind. You must be more assertive. If you wake up in the morning and your dreams have told you that you are to fall in love that day, then you must believe them. When you smile at the handsome and rich men who come to buy your carrots, you must do so in a way which makes it clear to them that you are certain that this is your day. So tell me, did your dreams tell you last night that this is your day?' She answered 'No' and said that instinct had deserted her because she no longer trusted it. Like a hurt friend it had given her up because she ignored it and called it names when she went to bed at night. Rory Brophy told her that clearly they were not meant for each other, but that she must renew her faith in the most unscientific of sciences. When they parted, the melancholy woman, whose name he never found out, presented Rory with a carrot to chew, for no man should have an empty stomach on such an important day.

The faces of women have done many things in history. They have started wars and launched ships. New religions have emerged on the backs of women's faces (forgive the phrase). Rory Brophy knew that there was a face in the city that day which would cause him to behave in a strange fashion. He did not think he would be at war by midnight because of it. A launched ship was also out of the question in such a short time, and the possibility that he might found a new religion could be immediately dismissed. What happened was quite different: by midnight on the 'Thursday of Love' Rory Brophy had taken to memorising the first sentences of the great works of literature. 'What on earth for?' I asked him. 'Because it was easier than learning the whole books,' he said. 'Now shut up and listen.'

After he had taken the carrot from the hawker, he walked through the city waiting for his big encounter. It was difficult for him not to try to induce fate. He wanted to go and sit beside a pretty woman who was sipping coffee in a restaurant. He also wanted to bump into an equally pretty woman who was carrying groceries. If he caused her to drop the packages and then offered to carry them for her as repayment, he would surely make an impression. But that was how things happened in fiction; this was real life, and to deliberately cause such a meeting would bring no rewards. So he could only do what instinct told him to. This in itself created problems, for he was seldom sure when it was prompting him and when not. Because he believed that the chance for perfect love occurred only once, he was terribly nervous that he might miss it by doing something he did not instinctively want to do. Even the call of nature was problematic. He knew he should only want to go a few times in the day, but thinking about this made him want to go more often. Large, gaping urinals kept looming up in front of him, calling him. This was unnatural. Such a thought might make him go to the toilet in a bar, and while he was there the woman who would bring him perfect bliss might pass by and their paths would never cross again. Being natural became very difficult. He questioned every urge he had: whether to turn left or right? To walk faster or slower? Rory Brophy felt that he could look the wrong way and condemn himself to a life of loneliness.

Rory Brophy's instinct had him walking at four o'clock in the afternoon in a part of the city where the streets were narrow and lined with shops. The hours since he had spoken to the carrot lady had been difficult. He had been given no sign that he was close to finding this woman. In fact it appeared to him that the women he had passed that day had been bad-tempered and unfriendly. Some of them had bumped into him and not apologised. But in this part of the city he saw a young woman through the window of a bookshop. She was arguing with an old man about the price of a second-hand book on rambling in Lithuania. Rory Brophy stood rooted to the pavement as if his feet had been set in the concrete. He was mesmerised by the accuracy of his waters' prediction. Like a salmon that returns to the same place to spawn after roaming the Atlantic, Rory Brophy had this innate sense that destiny had drawn him to this spot to witness the beauty of this young woman arguing over the trivial matter of the price of a book.

He did not wish to embarrass her when she was dealing with a customer by confronting her and announcing himself as her lover for eternity, or until one of them died, so he decided to wait for the frugal old man to leave before walking into her world. He crossed to the far side of the street as he did not want her to see him peering in the window and become alarmed about his intentions. While standing on the opposite side of the street, he saw a priest walk up and enter the shop. This annoyed him because he now had to wait longer. The thrifty old man left with his book under his arm and the priest began to speak to the girl. Rory Brophy shuffled his feet and wished the man of God would do his business and leave. While the priest was still speaking to the girl, Rory saw a man of about forty walk in the direction of the shop and he could tell by looking at him that he was a man who read a lot. Rory was right. The man stood and looked in the window, then entered the shop. Rory Brophy was furious with him because he was getting cold standing about and was anxious to fulfil his fate. He could be there for hours if things went on the way they were.

The priest soon left with a bag under his arm and Rory Brophy decided that he had been waiting long enough. Even if the man still inside overheard his conversation with his new love, he would understand. People who read books are intelligent and intelligence is a form of love; intelligent people know what it is to love. Rory explained to me that he was existing in another world as he crossed the street. He was without any feelings of shyness or doubt. He was so certain that what he was doing was right that he had no fear as he entered the bookshop, walked up to the girl and announced to her that they were in love and one day they would be married. 'She was a bit surprised by my statement,' he said to me, 'but I reassured her that when I had woken that morning, lying behind the skip of construction sand, I had been clear in my mind that this was the day for which my heart had been given to me, and that by midnight a great union would have taken place, that my spirit and that of a woman would be perched together on a branch like two love-birds. There was no question about it, I told her, my waters never lied when it came to my brilliant Thursdays. My instincts were never wrong on these days. She could bet her ancestral collection of chinaware on my waters when they spoke to me about my magnificent Thursdays.'

Before either of them could say another word, the

intellectual man went out into the street sniggering with laughter and ran off with his hand covering his mouth. 'Pay no attention to him,' said Rory to the girl. 'Intellectuals know nothing about love.' He then went on to tell her about his belief that the chance for perfect love only comes once. He enquired if she had woken that morning with any sense of expectancy about the day. She replied that she had, but only because it was her pay day. 'Forgive me if I disappoint you,' she said to him, 'but I am certain that I am not in love with you. I have never met you before. I don't know your name and I don't believe in love at first sight.' Rory Brophy told her that he was relieved about the last bit, given his ridiculous physique. 'We have nothing in common,' she said. 'Now excuse me, but you have to go, I must close the shop.'

Rory Brophy recalled that he heard those last words, 'I must close the shop,' as a stooge hears the click of the hypnotist's fingers. 'All of a sudden I was back in the real world,' he said. 'It was as if a different person had walked into the shop and said what I had said. Now I was having to explain that stranger's behaviour.' It was more than he could do. He could not stand there; instead he ran out the door and down the street. He ran so fast he reached speeds close to those of the Thursday of Speed. He ran and he cried. He was crying for himself and his own stupidity; for the way God had made him so different that he could not be part of the normal world. 'You bastard,' he said to himself, 'you silly bastard. Look what you've done. Look what a fool you've made of yourself.' He desperately wanted to go back to the shop. He could imagine the young woman laughing to herself at the very minute he was running like a chicken from the scene of his absurdity. How she would enjoy recounting to her friends, in exact detail, the story of the madman who had come into her shop that day and told her that his waters had predicted that they were in love. She might even add things that had not actually happened, accentuating his craziness, exaggerating his pathetic physique, until all her friends roared with laughter and accompanied each other home in case they met the anorexic Romeo. This was as much as he could take. He could not bear to have her go home thinking that way. He had to return and explain to her that he was sane, and that the clumsiness of his initial introduction had just been the result of his nerves getting the better of him. The idea that she would sleep that night without him having explained himself was unthinkable. He couldn't have her lying in bed for hours pondering his behaviour. So he turned around, dried his eyes and began to run back to the shop. But he was too late. When he reached it the door was locked and no amount of banging on the window would bring anyone out to answer him. The shop was empty. This was calamitous. He had missed the one opportunity of his life for real love.

This was a terrible day for Rory Brophy, the first time that his brilliant Thursdays had gone wrong. His waters had been right in that he had met the woman he loved; but they had not taken account of the possibility that she might feel differently. He cursed his chauvinistic frame of mind for having manufactured such a terrible disappointment for him.

That night he returned to the space behind the skip of construction sand, half hoping that he would experience a sequel to his feeling of that morning. Perhaps some residue of his brilliant Thursdays might still be found there. He might have missed something in the euphoria that had engulfed him earlier, something to explain how love was not like mathematics or speed or song. He lay in the position he was sure he had woken in that morning when his waters had spoken to him, and sure enough he began to hear them again. They were telling him that it was impossible to love in just one day. You had to be patient with it. A day was too short. This advice made him feel better, and then he remembered something she had said to him about them not having anything in common.

This was how Rory Brophy took to memorising the first lines of the great works of fiction. Such a talent was sure to impress her. Just imagine someone possessing such knowledge, he thought to himself. How impressive he would appear when he asked her to name her favourite great novel and was then able to recite to her the opening line. An original party trick for her well-read friends! Far more unusual than boring old singers and joke-tellers. She would be proud of him when people marvelled at his knowledge, and then she would love him.

At the hour before dawn Rory Brophy sat at the top of the mound of construction sand and watched for the sun to come up (he was very good at waiting). He thought to himself that he would go to one of the big bookshops in the city and spend the day there. By that night, he would have expanded his knowledge considerably, and after a few weeks he felt he would be ready to return to his woman and begin reciting opening lines to her, so that it would be clear that they shared a great interest in literature.

By nine o'clock he was sitting on the steps of the

biggest bookshop in Stockholm. He was the first customer to pass through the doors when they opened,
and he commenced his work immediately. His presence throughout the morning was noticed by the
shop manager, who came to him and asked him what
he was up to. Rory told him that he was in the process
of becoming a genius, an entertainer of the highest
calibre who would be admired by men and loved by
women, but that there was only one woman whose
love he wanted. 'Very soon we will share a common
knowledge of literature,' said Rory. 'Lovers must have
things in common, you know.' The shop manager
appeared to be stunned by this reply and apologised
to Rory for interrupting such important work; but
Rory assured him that no apology was necessary. He
even brought Rory a chair to sit on and a cup of tea
and a ham sandwich at lunchtime. This man became
Rory's patron during the four days that he sat in front
of the shelves and memorised opening line after opening line. It was the most intense period of intellectual
activity he had ever experienced, yet the learning
came easily to him. In the evenings he would return to
the skip where the residue of the Thursday of Love
still lingered in the air.

At the end of the fourth day of his study, Rory
Brophy returned the chair to the shop manager and
thanked him for his generosity. He told him that he
would not be coming back again as he believed he was
sufficiently prepared. 'May it always be Thursday for
you, Sir,' he said to him. The shop manager did not
understand this, but Rory told him that he hoped they
would meet again some day when he would have the
pleasure of introducing him to his beautiful wife. On
this last night behind the skip before returning to his

woman, Rory Brophy spent the hours rehearsing the first lines of the classics of literature. He confused many of them, but went to sleep with the belief that this was the last night of his life that he would spend in a state of loneliness. In the morning he went to the bookshop and stood at the door, where he saw her loading books about South American insects on to shelves.

'My father's name being Pirrip, and my Christian name being Philip, my infant tongue could make of both names nothing longer or more explicit than Pip,' he said. She stopped loading the shelves and stared at him in amazement. 'Call me Ishmael,' he continued. She did not reply. 'You do not know me, without you have read a book by the name of *The Adventures of Tom Sawyer*, but that ain't no matter.' Rory confessed to me that she remained fixed in a stare and showed no signs of emotion. He wasn't quite sure if this was amazement at his talent or not, so he tried again. 'Ah bien, mon prince, so Genoa and Lucca are now no more than private estates of the Bonaparte family.' He could see that she was still in a state of paralysis, so he thought he had better stop before he injured her with his knowledge. 'I suppose you thought I was insane the other day when I came in and told you that we were in love,' he said to her. It was only then that she returned to normal and put the books on South American insects down on the ground. 'I'm not mad, you know. I can quote the opening line of every great novel you wish to name. There isn't a mad person who can do that. Every night since I met you I have lain down and thought about you and the more I do, the more I know I am right. You should always trust your instinct, you know. And we have so much in common, you and I.'

In the minutes that followed she admitted that she had not considered him mad when he had said the things he had to her. Indeed, she had been a little flattered because it was the first time anyone had said such things to her in such a genuine way. 'Most men say things like that because they want you to go to bed with them, but I had a feeling that that was not the case with you. I don't think the idea of sleeping with me has crossed your mind.' 'You're absolutely right,' said Rory. 'I hadn't thought about that at all and I don't mean it as an insult. It's just that I am still a virgin through neglect more than failure. How about this one: "Gregory, on my word, we'll not carry coals".'

In the days that followed, Rory Brophy returned to the shop frequently. It was a strange affair because he limited their contact to the daytime, as he had no money to take her anywhere in the evenings. She consumed almost his entire thoughts. She came to him at the most unromantic of moments: the time a tramp vomited beside him in the early hours of the morning, or when he saw a dog shit on the pavement. Even at such times he thought of her, and this convinced him that he was truly in love. 'Only real love could be present in such circumstances and survive,' he would say to himself. 'You see, my beautiful Abby, the thought of you makes even the most disgusting sights bearable.' But he never told her this. Although he considered it complimentary to her that her image sanitised these filthy things, he thought it best not to mention it to her at this stage in case she took offence. So instead he told her that she came to him when he saw beautiful things like the paintings in the gallery, or the hills of leaves that fell from the trees. She was pleased at this, but still Rory looked forward to the day when he could tell her of the less pleasant sights which evoked her image in his mind.

These were the greatest days in the history of Rory Brophy. He was an explorer of love, going through feelings he had never believed himself capable of. He told me that his whole perception of man was changed by this woman. He had not thought we were able to reach such states of pleasure as those he felt when he lay behind the sand-filled skip with the tramps vomiting around him, and everything evoking her image. 'Such nights of bliss,' he said to me. 'Darkness has such a special gift when it comes to matters of love.'

Rory Brophy told me this tale as we sat in a bar owned by a woman called Phillippa Kerley, who could open bottles of beer with her nostrils and yodelled Sibelius to entertain her customers. Her rendition of 'Finlandia' was famed throughout the city, but she reserved it for special occasions. She had performed it only five times in the previous two years. Four had been as celebrations: the birth of her nephew, the marriage of her brother, the graduation of her sister from medical college, and a famous victory by Sweden in soccer. The fifth performance had taken place on the occasion of her betrayal by a lover. People said he was interested in her only for her money. Some of her best friends confided amongst themselves that, although she was a woman capable of great devotion, no man could love a woman who opened beer bottles with her nostrils. She did not heed their subtle warnings and fell hopelessly for a man called Irvine Border, who told her that she was at her most beautiful when she had a bottle up her nose. This was one of the ways Irvine Border used to work his way into her heart. 'He had a tongue like a snake,' said Ernest Knee, who sat beside us. 'He could slither through the tiniest gap with it, all the way into Phillippa's confidence, and that's a long, narrow road.' The day that had been predicted by her friends came for Phillippa Kerley as she planned the occasion of the second anniversary of the day Irvine Border had strolled into her bar and picked the lock of her heart with his tongue. Only two weeks short of this day they had made love on a bed above the bar, and in a moment of forgetfulness, he had called out the name of another woman. 'It's my mother,' he pleaded, 'it's my mother. When I suck your breasts it brings me back to my poor mother, God rest her soul.' But Phillippa Kerley was not fooled and she told him that a man with a tongue like his could never love his mother. 'I would not be surprised if you deceived her as a child the way you have done me. Did you creep on to the bosom of her best friend, you two-faced liar?' Before he could get out of the room, she proceeded to break the tops of all his fingers by inserting them up her nose and twisting her head. Just like she did when she opened bottles.

That evening there was a sense of tragedy and expectancy in Phillippa Kerley's bar. Although she did not show her true emotions, or make any reference to an impending performance, whispers were exchanged to the effect that a happening of extraordinary beauty would take place after she had closed the doors and gone up to her room. 'Don't go home tonight,' was the advice given, 'we think she will yodel.' When everyone had left and she was alone, Phillippa Kerley went up to her room, oblivious to the presence of dozens of people standing outside in the street in silence and waiting to feast their ears. They were not to be disappointed; they had been well advised. Just before one o'clock she began to yodel 'Finlandia.' People fell to their knees because their legs would not support them. What a performance it was that night! In the morning she found the dried up tracks of tears on the glasses that were lined up neatly on the pavement outside her bar.

Because Rory Brophy had become a regular in her establishment, Phillippa Kerley had promised him that she would yodel something special on the occasion of the birth of his child. It would not be 'Finlandia' as she reserved that for personal occasions, but it would be a tribute to his new child. Phillippa Kerley told me of the first time she had ever met Rory.

It was around midday when he came in. 'He was full of life,' she remembered. 'He came up to me and said that he hoped I was having a good day. In fact he turned to the few people who were here and wished them all a good day.' This was not long after her betrayal by Irvine Border, so she was wary of him. 'At that time in my life I considered nothing to be more dangerous than a stranger in a good mood who wished me good day.' He then told her that he had recently fallen deeply in love. She felt sorry for him when she heard this. 'In those days there was nothing more pathetic to me than a soul that was deeply in love,' she said. 'I warned him intensely. I felt like a banshee predicting a death. I quizzed him about who had made the first move. If it had not been him he was in grave danger; there is nothing more vulnerable than the lover who does not make the first move. The one who speaks first is always the one who is aware of what will follow. Whoever speaks second relies on trust.'

What Phillippa Kerley most remembered about her early encounters with Rory Brophy was the way he began to rehabilitate her after the events with Irvine Border. 'It would not be an exaggeration to say that at the time I met Rory Brophy I was at the lowest point in my life. The hands of my clock were at half-six, my enthusiasm was at absolute zero.' By her description of her state then (which still made her eyes well up), I could see that she had been very lucky to have had the lunatic-in-love Rory Brophy come through the doors of her business. She summed up her condition in one phrase: 'I was a corpse in waiting,' she said. She had considered closing her bar. It was becoming too much of a struggle for her to make conversation with her customers. She had lost all interest in them. 'For a person in my trade that is the death-knell,' she said. 'If you run a bar, you not only have to be able to serve a good drink to a man, you also have to be able to listen to him when he tells you he no longer loves his wife and is having an affair with another woman. You have to be his wet-nurse, his psychiatrist and his adviser. If you can't do that, if you tell him to go drown himself when he begins to disclose his problems to you, then you are no longer any good at your job. You should be struck off. You might as well retire to the country and paint watercolours until you die.' Phillippa Kerley confessed that at the time she first met Rory Brophy she was considering such a course. What was so difficult for her was that her anguish was so public. 'Everyone knew about it,' she said. 'When I broke down in tears at the slightest problem, I could sense them all murmuring beneath their breaths "We warned you, Phillippa, we did warn you." ' I felt like a patient after a heart transplant who has had the walls of her room removed so everyone could look at her and chart the course of her recovery. No one could convalesce under such circumstances, and that was how I felt. I thought it was the end for me. I don't know how many customers I insulted when they asked me to listen to their woes, but I just had not got it in me to be interested in them. They could have dropped dead as they sat on a stool in front of me and I probably would have done nothing more than drag them outside like they had died of a plague.'

Phillippa Kerley's chance meeting with Rory Brophy might well have saved her life. 'It was his sheer, boundless energy which I found renewing,' she said. 'His happiness, his confidence that he was not mistaken in the matter of this woman. Too much happiness for him to handle himself. He was like a chemist's beaker bubbling over. It was so infectious. People would say to me when they came in, "Has The Poet been in yet?" ' (This was because he would recite the first lines of famous books to them and was erroneously named 'The Poet' because of it.) 'He cheered everyone up,' said Phillippa. 'It was as if we were all falling in love as well. It would not be a lie for me to say that there was something spiritual about it. He seemed to give a new lease of life to the practice of love. You understand that many of the men who come in here are married and this is the only way they can get away from their wives. Even some of these men began to change due to the healing effect of Rory Brophy's enthusiasm about love. They no longer asked me to understand their problems. Some of them even began to bring their wives in with them. For me, the arrival of this Rory Brophy was a salvation. My customers began to comment on it. "You're in much better form these days, Phillippa," they would say. In the first few months that I knew him, I could feel the curtain being slowly lowered on the past, and there was Rory in the wings pulling on the rope. And he kept on doing so until I could no longer see behind it. He is a very important person to me,' she said.'He is very special, you are lucky to have such a friend.'

I find it hard to understand now the arrogance of my mission in Stockholm. As I listened to Phillippa Kerley speak to me of her encounters with Rory and to all the greetings that were extended to him by her customers, the magnitude of my mistake began to upset me. When we left the bar and walked through the back streets, more people called out his name and wished him a good day and good health. 'Tell your beautiful wife that she should not be working in her condition,' said a man called Stefan Wainwright, who owned a pawnbroker's shop. 'I passed by there the other day and I could not believe my eyes. Pat her on the belly and say hello to the baby for me as well, will you?' In the space of fifteen minutes' walking we must have met six or seven people who suggested names for the baby. There was the little fat man with the dirty brown overcoat who was picking his nose when we passed him on the far side of the street. He did not see us until we had our backs to him, and then he called out, 'Hey, Rory Brophy, do you know that myself and all my brothers are called after rivers? My two sisters are called after mountains. This was my late mother's idea, because she always said that the source of a good man was a good woman. Keep that in mind when it comes to naming your baby, won't you. I've been thinking that if it's a boy you could call him Danube, that way he could be nicknamed Danny. If it's a girl, then I think Fuji would sound great . . . Fuji Brophy. I'm not trying to force you, but my mother was no idiot. She lived to be ninety-four. When she died, we were all present to witness it. It was like a geography lesson when she spoke to us. She was in full command of her faculties as well as having all her teeth, so she was a woman who knew what she was talking about.' 'Thank you, Elbe,' said Rory, 'I will give it some thought.'

Other people just called out names to him. 'What about Suzanna, Rory?' or 'It's got to be Rodrigo,' or 'I think Manus is a great name.' Even now, at a time when all of this is a few years old, I can still hear the voices of those people who had come to know Rory well enough to stop their business and stand in the street yelling names at him. I have spoken before about how I had not developed a feeling of jealousy towards Rory. That was before. I have been attempting to portray myself as the model citizen (and in many respects I think I am), but I admit that it was while walking amidst the noise of names that my resistance finally broke down and I was overcome by intense jealousy which made me look at my friend with eyes that wished him bad luck. Things were going just too well for him. It was an ordeal even for a basically decent person like myself to have to watch all these wonderful events unfold for him. My pleasure in reflected happiness was waning and it was more than I could bear. I was unaware at that time that my sensibility had been affected by the hours of drinking at Phillippa Kerley's, but I felt like speaking my mind. 'Rory,' I said to him, 'I'm just fed up with all these good things happening to you. I'm sick and tired of it. It's unnatural for someone to experience such good fortune. It's unhealthy even. This is the real world, you know. You're the same person that people used to beat up without giving it a second thought. There's nothing I would enjoy more right now than to see it happen again. Just don't get too cocky, do you hear? Don't think that Old Mother Bad Luck has forgotten you. Apples grow big and juicy so they can be picked and eaten, and you're a big red apple hanging on a low branch and someone in the garden is hungry.'

Rory Brophy was very amused by my outburst. 'You're drunk,' he said. 'I've never seen you jealous before. You're quite good at it, you know. I don't know how that is because it's not a normal state for you, but don't be jealous of me. Don't think I have forgotten things. Go and ask Abby about the number of times I wake up at night singing. I have this terrible habit of singing in my sleep. Not because I'm happy, but because it makes me forget. It diverts my mind when it begins to drift back to the past. I woke up one morning singing "This Nearly Was Mine" because I had been dreaming about the time Softy Mullen rubbed toothpaste into my hair. I must be turning a mental switch, but one minute I'm fast asleep having a nightmare and the next minute I'm sitting up singing.'

I can tell you now that he was not joking about this singing. Despite the good things that happened, in the nights that followed, my sleep was periodically disturbed by outbursts of singing.

That same night I was sound asleep beneath the influence of alcohol, dreaming about the day that

227

Lazy Uncle Kevin had been involved in an exercise most energetic for him, when his precious and beloved deck-chair collapsed beneath his untoned flab. He jumped to his feet looking in all directions, thinking that his most prized possession had been sabotaged. The sight of the tangled piece of furniture almost reduced him to tears. The prospect of life without his deck-chair was terribly traumatic. He actually ran to the house of the master craftsman Ivan Youkstetter. It was during this journey that both his feet left the ground simultaneously for the first time since his marriage (with the exception of when he went to bed). Ivan Youkstetter found Lazy Uncle Kevin in such a state of distress that he immediately asked him what had happened to his deck-chair. 'It's in bits,' said my distraught uncle, 'collapsed into smithereens beneath me. Please help me.' Ivan Youkstetter managed to repair the chair within two hours, but the whole affair put a terrific strain on Lazy Uncle Kevin and he was overcome by exhaustion that evening. He dozed in a condition which the summoned doctor described as 'supersleep'. The patient did not emerge from his coma for three and a half days, upon which he immediately announced that he thought he would take a nap. This may appear slightly amusing now, but at the time it was a matter of grave concern to Auntie Beatrice because, despite how little contact they had during their marriage, it was one of those partnerships in which real affection exists like a water-table beneath the surface. This is what I dreamt about the night following my outburst of jealousy, and this was what was interrupted by the abominable sound of Rory Brophy singing 'Come Into The Garden, Maude'.

His constant musical interruptions made sleep difficult to come by that night, so I was tired the following morning when Rory reminded me that he and Abby would be married a week from that day. A delay had been caused by the refusal of her mother to attend her eldest daughter's wedding because she was not a virgin. There had never been a wedding in the family where everyone could see as plain as day that the bride was not intact, and that her white robes concealed a lie. Being the mother of such a bride was something that Abby's mother would not consent to. 'I saw it in her mouth the moment I laid eyes on her,' Rory said to me, 'before we had even told her that Abby was pregnant and wished to marry me.' Abby had taken Rory to dinner at her parents' house. Her father seemed shocked when Rory entered the house, but after a short while he gathered himself again and shook hands violently, explaining his belief that the first handshake was very important in a friendship. Abby's mother was not so warm. 'You should have seen her mouth,' Rory repeated. 'Some day I must take you to see it. It's like a doughnut. Big, puffy lips with a hole in the middle for complaining. She has the mouth of a snob if I ever saw one.' The seeds of trouble to come were evident in her mouth that evening, clear as if she had chewed them and spat them out all over Rory's diamondy jersey. Rory reckoned that her mouth had already sensed that three people were coming to dinner. It seemed to have a brain of its own, to exist independently of the rest of her body – an intelligent tumour on her face which could detect trouble before it was made apparent. Abby's mother had not come around to accepting the invitation to her daughter's wedding, and had even forbidden her other daughters to attend and witness the sight of a pregnant woman walking to the altar. They had put the wedding off as long as they could in the hope that she would have a change of heart, but she had not, so they would go ahead without her.

I have never been to one before, but I can safely say that my experience of this famous day in the life of Rory Brophy left me with the opinion that weddings are terrific. Seeing Abby in white was a revelation. If I were to pretend to be clever about this I would say that a woman looks better in white than she does naked, but that would be getting carried away. However, she did look beautiful. After the wedding ceremony we went to a room above the café of Riocard Bentley, which he rented to couples who could not afford the high prices charged by the big hotels. The room was long and narrow with a fine view of the docks – not the most picturesque view imaginable, although a large volume of water does have a way of looking good no matter where it is. In the earlier part of the day, Abby had been a little upset. I imagined it was because events were overtaking her so quickly. Perhaps she also felt she had been deserted by her family, none of whom came because her mother had forbidden it. Abby must have felt guilty that her own happiness had been such a divisive issue, but her sorrow passed as the day progressed and she began to laugh and sing a little more.

Still, it was all bitter-sweet for her. She told me when I danced with her that she had been unsure all day of whether to laugh or cry. 'Sometimes it all gets too much for me,' she said. 'I wish it was all over and there was just the three of us living in our own apartment.' (By this she meant herself, Rory and their

new child. I realised this just in time to avoid making a
fool of myself by insisting that I had no place in their
lives besides being a good friend, which I hoped I
would always remain.)

I have to say, and do not get me wrong, that the
hour I spent talking to her that night was the most
memorable of all the time I had spent in Stockholm. It
was a conversation during which I discovered a true
friend. This is a great event when it happens, and rare,
too, which makes it all the more special. I told her I
was delighted she had met Rory because I had spent a
lot of time worrying about him. Fate had given him to
me as a neighbour in the same stroke that it had given
me a conscience that worried about underdogs more
than was good for any man. She had been my saviour
in the case of Rory. I told her that at one time I had felt
he was such a helpless case that I would have to marry
him myself.

For myself, I had guessed that I would be all right. I
was no freak of nature. Women had never shown any
signs of being repulsed by me, so I reckoned that one
day a girl would walk into my life and we would live
happily ever after. I knew that when that day came I
would invite Rory Brophy to my wedding, perhaps
even make him my best man, although this would be
likely to cause framing difficulties for the photo-
grapher. But there I would be on my wedding day,
dancing with my mother-in-law and sisters-in- law,
persistently spying out of the corner of my eye and
seeing my lifelong friend Rory Brophy sitting in the
corner on his own. That was how I had always
thought it would be, but I had been wrong. Now, here
was I where I had imagined he would be.

He did not have a mother-in-law to dance with. She

had deemed his relationship with her daughter in the time before their marriage to be wholly disgraceful and would most certainly not be caught in the act of dancing with a man so impatient when it came to the matter of consummation. She had also denied him a dance with his sisters-in-law. No dance with Christine, the intellectual one, who loved books more than men. No dance with Silvina, the youngest one, who ate onions like they were apples. No dance with Petra, who had told Rory that she thought him the luckiest person she knew because he was marrying her sister. She believed that her older sister (by eighteen months) was the prettiest of the family. If it were not for the tradition of not falling in love with your sister, she said to him, she would have fallen in love with Abby. 'What dreadful things traditions are,' she confessed to Rory, 'that they make you afraid to do the things you most want to do. Tradition will have me marry a man I love far less than I do my sister. What is so wrong with loving your own flesh and blood? Where did this stupid rule come from? Who was the man who so hated his sister that he framed this rule and denied the rest of us such pleasure?'

Rory had always considered Petra a little odd. She had a habit of confronting him with the most extreme scenarios. She asked him if her sister was good to sleep with. What sounds did she make, did she utter non-words of ecstasy, or was she coherent when she had an orgasm? He refused to answer these questions, telling her that he did not think they should talk about such things. She persisted, telling him that he could sleep with her if he would tell her what she wanted to know. He still refused and they had an argument, which remained unresolved. Petra barely maintained civility towards Rory Brophy. She was not able to display outright hostility towards him without giving away her true feelings, but she told him what she had to tell and then retreated to play the role that the man who hated his sister had decreed she should play.

Even though he had none of these women to dance with, nor the hand of a father-in-law to shake, Rory Brophy had a day to beat all days, even his brilliant Thursdays. In the morning he dressed himself in a hat and tails. 'For the first time in my life I look handsome,' he said as we looked at him in the bedroom mirror. He was unnerved by the wedding ceremony which he dismissed as having too much praying in it. It was only when he sat at the window in the room above Riocard Bentley's café that he relaxed. From there he could turn his head around and look out at the harbour where a ship of satsumas had once come in with a stowaway on board. He smiled all day from then on. The pictures which were taken of him showed him laughing with his big mouth open. 'It's the only part of me that isn't skinny,' he said.

When the day was over, Rory and Abby went to spend their first night in their new apartment, which we had finished decorating at half past ten the previous evening. There was a wonderful smell of fresh paint in it which Rory pronounced to be an aphrodisiac whose powers he would have to control, given that he would be a father in a few days. They lived next door to a man called Carl Satie, who in turn lived next door to Isobel and Marcus Freud, who were in their sixties. They reassured Rory that they were no relation to the great psychoanalyst; however Marcus Freud did indulge in bouts of amateur behavioural interpretation. His subject was his wife, who was

paranoid about security. She had a habit of memorising the locks and bolts on the doors of houses she
entered. Marcus Freud had never let his wife know
that he was studying her, but he had tried for many
years to get her to talk about her past to see if he could
pin-point an occasion on which her security had been
breached, giving rise to her unusual habit. He told
Rory Brophy that he had still not isolated the incident,
or incidents. He had surreptitiously questioned her
about break-ins to her house when she was a child.
She could not remember any. She had never been
assaulted either. There appeared to be no occasion on
which her safety had even been threatened. He had
then delved into the murkier waters of family relations. He had engaged her in long conversations
about her father. He had died before Marcus Freud
had met her, and there was an awful possibility that
things had happened between father and daughter
that ought not to have happened, and which drew the
eyes of the woman to the locks and bolts on every
door that closed behind her. She memorised them all.
Her sister Bertha's apartment had one mortise lock
and a small bolt at the bottom. The door of the
apartment of Missus Francesca Crilly, which was sit-
uated above the cake shop where Isobel Freud went
for tea every Friday evening, had one mortise lock, a
chain and a large bolt at the top. The door of the
rector's house had only one mortise lock. When they
went for tea with friends in the evenings, her first
comments to her husband on leaving would be about
any new locks that might have been fitted since their
last visit. When their first grandchild was born, she
gave the infant what she called a 'christening lock',
which was to be kept and placed on the first door that

the child would call her own. This was the way that the mind of Isobel Freud worked. She told Rory Brophy one evening, when the doctor had come to see Abby, that he ought to get a chain for the door, and one bolt to be placed at the top.

I had told Rory that I would stay in Stockholm until the child was born. Eight days after their wedding, he came to my apartment in the morning and told me that he had been to the hospital with Abby and she had been advised to stay. He was upset with excitement. 'Can you imagine,' he said to me, 'in a few hours' time I will be a father . . . me, the rake, a father.' I hid my own excitement as best I could as it was his prerogative to do the panicking. He drank so much coffee that he was sick in the toilet a few doors away from where Abby lay. I have to say that in those hours he became closer to the old Rory Brophy who had jumped off the flyover. He struck me as being very vulnerable, in the way that happy people often are. I gave up trying to keep pace with him as he walked up and down the hospital corridor, wringing his hands till the blood almost oozed from them. It seemed like we were very close to a fine new future. So close, yet still at a point of fragile suspension. We were at the point when the new vase is being taken carefully from its box and placed on the cabinet. When the birthday cake is carried from the kitchen with trembling hands. We were approaching the crest of the hill, about to see over the top, at the point where a slip would reveal how far there was to fall. Rory came and sat beside me. I brought him some tea and he was complaining that there was too much milk in it when a nurse came up to him and said that he was the father of a son who weighed eight pounds and couldn't half scream.

I'm not quite sure who was hugging who in the minute that followed the nurse's announcement. I was hugging him for sure, but he also seemed to be congratulating me. Perhaps it was the shock that made him lose track of the situation, but it did seem that he was so overcome that he forgot what he was overcome about. I was the one who asked the nurse if we could go and see the mother and child. 'Great idea,' said Rory, and we were led to their room.

What a meeting that was for us. I would have stayed longer but felt that it was not my place, so I left the three of them and returned to the seat in the corridor where I had prayed and been answered. Rory came out to me after thirty minutes, on the instructions of the midwife, and we went and found a bar where I bought him a drink with some money he had given me. I toasted him for having made it all the way from the flyover to here. He told me how he had thought of inviting his greatest tormentors of old to witness this occasion – the ones who had filled his trousers with sand from the long-jump pit and blown smoke in his face, and the ones who had taken his trousers off him in the sheds and made him run to the bottom of the yard and back before returning them to him. He had thought how sweet it would be to have them witness this triumphant occasion. But then he informed me that the previous night he had vowed to himself that if everything went well for himself and Abby, and the child was delivered safely, he would expel all thoughts of revenge from his mind and would forgive them all. Things had gone well, so he raised a glass of vodka above his head and absolved them all, wishing them a happy life.

We were very drunk when I got him back to his apartment that night and put him to bed. The following morning his hangover hardly troubled him as he left for the hospital telling me that he would pick up some flowers on the way. 'You will have to stay for the christening,' he shouted to me as he went out the door. 'It will be in a few days' time. Don't worry about money, I am a wealthy man now.' You will know if you have ever been close to people you love when they have a child that it is perhaps the most wonderful thing that can happen to a man and a woman. I have already spoken about the cleansing effect that such an event has. It is difficult for me to write about how good it all felt at that time. You will understand it if you have experienced it; if you haven't, then it is something you must seek out.

A week after she had given birth, Abby returned home and had her wish of the three of them moving into their apartment with the view of the trees through the window. It was at this point that I decided I should make my exit and return home with a concocted story for those I had left in turmoil. I had no idea of what that might be – probably something about memory loss which would have them carting me off for brain examinations. But my departure was to be delayed.

If you are a lover of happy endings, perhaps you should take leave of me now and I thank you for reading what you have. However, to do so might

THE DISAPPEARANCE OF RORY BROPHY

leave you with a warped view of the nature of happiness and of this world we live in.

You must recall the conversation I had with Erno Wellbeloved, the author of westerns – in particular, his interest in the footsteps of dinosaurs on the banks of the Paluxy River in Texas. If you have forgotten, you might take time to refresh your memory, for it will be of assistance to you in reading what is left. The decision is yours, but I will press on from here.

The day Abby came back from the hospital they informed me that they had decided to call him Rory. This was unoriginal, but it was what they would do. Young Rory Brophy was christened the following day and I held him in my arms and remembered the case of Billy Cashin, who had been baptised and absolved of all his sins by the same man who could not allow his shrapnel-ridden body into the church because the Bishop had taken sides. I held young Rory Brophy and he was absolved without us understanding what it was he was being absolved of. But I held him as the water was poured over his head making him clean again. In the evening of his deliverance from sin, we toasted him, asking that life should be good to him and that knowledge and good health should not avoid him.

The following morning I went into the city to purchase my return ticket. It was a fine morning, so I walked back. Again, I was remembering: this time it was the long walk I had made when buying my ticket to come here in the first place. So much had happened since then. I can recall that the street on which they lived was very quiet when I reached it. There was no one about, not even the old ladies with their dogs.

I went up to the first floor, where I saw that the door of Isobel and Marcus Freud was wide open. This was strange for the door belonging to the woman with the fixation about security. Beside it, the door of Carl Satie was also open. Further on, the door of Rory Brophy stood ajar. I pushed it open and inside I was met by the faces of the Freuds, Carl Satie, Max Sponge and another man who I did not recognise. They were all standing in a huddle and they turned around in concert to face me when I came in. Sitting on the couch beside them, with his eyes in another world and his hands dropped down between his knees so they reached the floor, was my friend Rory Brophy. He made no gesture of recognition when I entered. No one said anything, there was just a sideward gesture in the direction of the bedroom door.

I went over and pushed it open. There on the bed sat Abby. She was rocking backwards and forwards with a small bundle in her arms. She was crying, though she made no noise. There was no sound in the room. I remember the quietness of the day. She rocked and the tears streamed down her face and dropped from her chin on to the tiny bundle in her arms. Her son lay motionless in her arms with a white face and purple lips. His eyes were closed. She kissed him many times on the forehead and the top of his skull whilst rocking him all the while. What in the world was the point of it all? Where was the reason for this? Why had we been taken to the top of the mountain only to be flung off the edge? For there in her arms lay the body of her week-old son. Young Rory Brophy was gone.

In the days that followed, Rory Brophy could only describe his feelings as like standing at the front of a huge wall which was longer than the one in China and higher than the sky. He could not see over it or around it and he wondered why it was that nobody had ever been able to explain why such a wall existed. Why was it that the greatest minds in the world – who had answered many difficult problems, who could tell how we were born and how we lived – could not explain the thing that troubled us most. Why had they not been able to explain such things through the ordering of numbers, so that if you took the time to devote yourself to the mastering of mathematics, you would one day be able to know why it was that such a pointless thing should happen as the death of a child in its first days. He was like a fly at a window, clamouring to get through to the far side and unable to understand why he couldn't, the reason obscured by transparency.

I could not help myself comparing the fate of young Rory Brophy to that of Oliver Moorken, the Servant of God, who had died at the age of ten and was now the recipient of the prayers of a thousand mothers beseeching him to intercede on their behalf. It seemed unfair to me that such a child should be remembered and not the tiny son of my good friend. Was it to be his fate that only those who had known about him in the few days of his life would be aware that he had ever existed? What would happen when they were gone? The world would become totally ignorant of the fact that he had been here and been robbed of his chance to leave his footprint in the banks of the Paluxy River. He might only be recalled for the few seconds that it took a camera-strewn traveller, wandering through a graveyard someday, to read the ancient stone. Was this to be the only way anyone would ever remember his existence?

I vowed that it would not. That is why you have read this story. You are now aware that young Rory Brophy did live. Don't forget him and all those like him. This is his footstep. Thank you, and may it always be Thursday for you.